# Springtime in Winnipeg

## A John Smyth Mystery (#4)

### by James R. Coggins

**Mill Lake Books**

Judson Lake House
PUBLISHERS

Mill Lake Books
An imprint of Judson Lake House Publishers
Abbotsford, BC
Canada
www.judsonlakehouse.net
www.coggins.ca


Printed by Lightning Source, distributed by Ingram


Cover design by Dean Tjepkema


ISBN 978-0-9881462-5-9

for mystery fans
and those who never knew they were;
for those to whom the Mystery has been revealed
and those who will be added to their number

Other John Smyth Mysteries:
*Who's Grace?*
*Desolation Highway*
*Mountaintop Drive*

# __Prologue__
## *April*

When spring finally arrives in Winnipeg, the residents have a tendency to believe that they have earned it. After enduring six months of snow and numbing cold, a winter more fierce than that experienced by the inhabitants of almost any other city on earth, they emerge like shell-shocked soldiers from trench warfare. They stumble into April, a month of melting snow, thawing rivers, oozing mud, and hopeful signs. Snow gives way to rain. Migrating birds appear on the rivers. The trees swell in anticipation of new leaves. The first crocuses appear above the earth. And the lifeless bodies of beautiful young women are discovered lying near the paths in the woods along the Assiniboine River next to Assiniboine University.

# Chapter 1
## *Monday, November 24*

"He's going to kill *Grace*!"

"Who?"

"*Grace.*"

"Who's Grace?"

"*Grace* magazine."

"What?" Ruby had not been paying attention.

John Smyth was short—barely five feet tall—and easy to overlook, even for Ruby, who had been married to him for fifteen years and was only an inch or two taller. John was frustrated enough without this.

Ruby looked up from the book she was reading. "Who's trying to kill Grace?"

"Johnson Pickering. And I didn't say he was *trying* to kill *Grace*. I said he was *going* to kill *Grace.*"

"I'm missing something."

"Yes. You're going to be missing *Grace*—and my salary."

"That's not much."

"No, but the magazine matters."

"I'm sorry. I was really lost in this book. If I promise to pay attention, will you explain what you're talking about?"

"Where have I been?"

"Don't you know?"

John was silent, exasperated.

"Oh, yes, you were at the quarterly meeting of the board executive."

"Johnson Pickering…"

"He's the new chairman of your board."

"Right." Now that Ruby was paying attention, John was picking up steam again. "Johnson Pickering is going to kill *Grace* magazine."

"Why would he want to do that? He's chairman of the board responsible for publishing *Grace.*"

"I don't think he *wants* to do that. I'm afraid he's *going* to do that because he doesn't know what he's doing."

"What's he doing?"

"*Grace* is the magazine for all the members of the Grace Evangelical churches in North America. The churches are like a family. But Johnson Pickering is a businessman and he wants to run the magazine more like a business."

"What does that mean?"

"*Grace* has always been a magazine that was open to all members of the church. Anyone who had something to say could submit it to the magazine, and we would consider publishing it. The people who sent us things weren't always great writers, and sometimes what they sent us needed a lot of editing, but we got fresh perspectives that way, and everybody in the denomination felt like it was their magazine. Average people in the church could relate to the articles because they were written by other average people in the church like them. Now Johnson Pickering wants us to use more professional writers."

"Did you explain to him that it doesn't matter if the writers are professional as long as the editor is professional and he can correct the mistakes in the articles?"

John's shoulders sagged. "That's the other problem. Pickering wants a more professional editor too."

"He's firing you?"

"Not exactly. He wants me to get a journalism degree."

"What's wrong with that?'

"*Grace* has never had an editor with a journalism degree. The board has always said that they want someone with good editing skills but also someone who loves God and the church. And when it came time to choose, they have always said it was more important to find someone who loved God and the church because someone who loved God and the church could always learn editing skills on the job, but you can't train somebody to love God."

"So they hired you, you loved God, you were already a good writer, you learned editing skills on the job, and you have always tried to edit the magazine according to professional standards."

"Right."

"So why don't you want to get a degree and improve your editing skills?"

"You think I should go back to school and get a degree?"

"Sure. Why not?"

"I guess so. Pickering says I can do it part-time and the board will pay for the tuition costs."

"Then why don't you want to do it?"

"I'm too old to go back to school."

"You're forty."

"That's old."

"I'm forty."

John thought quickly. "That's still young, isn't it?"

"Good thinking."

# Chapter 2

*Thursday, December 18*

Winnipeg, a sprawling city of two-thirds of a million people, sits at the eastern edge of the Canadian prairies at the junction of two broad, shallow, prairie rivers. The Red River, in reality a muddy brown, flows north from Minnesota through the Canadian province of Manitoba to eventually empty into the frigid, ice-strewn waters of Hudson Bay. The smaller Assiniboine River flows east across the vast Canadian prairies and empties into the Red River at Winnipeg.

Neither river was flowing now. It was December, in the heart of the long Winnipeg winter, and both were frozen solid and covered by a blanket of white snow. Paths and rectangles had been cleared here and there on the rivers for skating, but mostly in Winnipeg in mid-winter it was too cold even for that.

The main business district and the provincial legislative buildings were spread out along the north shore of the Assiniboine. The south shore was more refined. It boasted, from west to east, the extensive rolling lawns and trees of Assiniboine Park, an enclave of stately mansions owned by Winnipeg's wealthiest citizens, and the compact campus of Assiniboine University. On the east side of the campus were several hectares of wooded land, an "endowment" set aside originally for expansion of the university but preserved now in perpetuity as an incongruous piece of "wilderness" in the middle of the city—the result of an intense lobbying campaign by campus environmentalists. In actuality, it was mostly a place for students to get away from the pressure of academic life, wander along shaded paths, hold drinking parties, and make out under the bushes. Unable to expand into its intended space along the river, Assiniboine University had turned in on itself, the buildings pushed higher and closer together than seemed befitting for an institution dedicated to expanding horizons.

In a cluttered administrative office, his winter parka hanging open, John Smyth was sitting anxiously across the desk from a skinny, middle-aged woman with dark-rimmed glasses. Her slightly graying hair hung limply down to her shoulders, and she absentmindedly bunched the top of her cardigan sweater against her throat with her left hand.

Looking up from some papers, she sighed. "Really, Mr. Smyth, I don't know why you asked for a counseling session. Regular application and registration processes are supposed to all be handled over the internet."

Smyth stretched his neck. "I, uh, had some questions," he said, "and I wanted to talk to a person. I'm not really comfortable with using the internet for things like that…"

Miss Grambling rolled her eyes. "If you're not comfortable with the basic elements of modern technology, then how do you expect to be able to handle university work, Mr. Smyth?"

Smyth squirmed. "Do you mean you're not going to accept me?"

Miss Grambling looked down at the papers again and frowned. "I don't see…" she began. "Your BA and your *Master of Divinity degree*"—she said the last words with an odd inflection—are from Grace Bible College and Seminary in Medicine Hat, Alberta." She sniffed. "We don't normally give advanced credit for Bible college work. The standards at a university are much higher." She looked down at the papers again, then raised her head suddenly. "Mr. Smyth, are you over forty?"

"Yes," he stammered. "I turned forty last year."

"That explains it," she said. "You are a mature student." She said the words as one would say, "You are a drunk," or "You are a cockroach."

"Is that bad?"

She sniffed. "Mature students are evaluated by different criteria. This explains why you have been accepted into the third year of the BA in English and Journalism program. You have been given two years' credit for your previous academic work and your life experience."

Smyth brightened. "That's good, isn't it? So what do I do next?"

"The credits are applied mainly to your electives. To obtain your BA, you will have to take an additional twenty courses in English and Journalism. This sheet lists all the required foundational courses, as well as the optional English and Journalism courses." She handed over a piece of paper. "And this sheet lists the courses available this term and the times they are offered." She handed over another sheet.

"Do I have to take the courses in any particular order?"

"No, Mr. Smyth, as long as you take all of the required courses, you can take them in any order you wish. However, you must maintain at least a B minus average to remain in the program."

Smyth had stopped listening. He was reading over the sheets. Maybe he should start with the English courses, he thought. English 329: The Mennonite Novel. English 337: The Life-Affirming Philosophy of Ernest Hemingway. English 341. Ah, that looked interesting. "Can I take English 341 this term?"

Miss Grambling looked at her copy of the sheets for a moment. "Yes, that would qualify as one of your senior English courses, and the course is not yet full. It's a course that is normally offered in the fall, but it was so popular that some students couldn't get in and the professor agreed to teach it as an extra evening class in the spring term."

"Spring term? I thought it was offered next term."

"Next term is the spring term. Spring term runs from January till April."

"Oh, okay. That's great. Sign me up for it."

"All right, but you will have to pay your fees in the business office down the hall."

"No problem," Smyth replied happily. "I'm having the tuition paid for me."

*****

"Next."

After seventeen minutes of standing impatiently in line, it was finally Smyth's turn. He walked up to one of the three wickets. A vacant-eyed woman with shoulder-length fuchsia hair and a nose ring stared absentmindedly over his head.

"I've come to pay my fees," Smyth said.

The woman sighed, took the printed form he had offered her, and began punching information into a computer terminal. After a couple of minutes, she punched a final key and stated in a low monotone, "Seven-sixty-three-forty-three."

"What?"

"Seven hundred and sixty-three dollars and forty-three cents."

Smyth looked confused. "But I'm only taking one three-hour course, and they told me that the fees were a hundred and eighty-seven dollars per credit hour. So that should be less than six hundred dollars."

The woman recited in the same monotone. "Three credit hours at a hundred-eighty-seven is five-sixty-one. Application fee fifty. Registration fee twenty-five per course. Library fee twelve dollars per course. Computer and internet fee eighteen per course. Student fee, half-rate for part-time students, ninety-seven-forty-three. Total seven hundred and sixty-three dollars and forty-three cents. Check, cash, debit, or credit card."

"What are all those fees? What is the…uh…student fee for, for instance?"

The woman recited again, "Clubs twenty-five, athletics twenty-seven-fifty, student union fourteen-fifty, student center mortgage twelve-twenty-one, Ambrosia Club mortgage eighteen-twenty-two."

"Ambrosia Club. What's the Ambrosia Club?"

"New student pub."

"I'm paying for a pub? I don't even drink."

"Compulsory fees. You don't pay the fees, you can't take the course."

Smyth pulled out his checkbook. He hoped there was enough money in the account to cover the check, and he hoped his family didn't need groceries before the denomination reimbursed him for the fees.

*****

"I'm in!" he shouted, coming through the door into the front hall.

"I know it's cold out," Ruby replied sardonically, "but you're not usually that excited about coming into the house."

"I mean at the university. I have been accepted into the third year of a BA in English and Journalism."

"Great," Ruby said.

"I take my first course next term, a three-hour class on Wednesday evenings. It's called 'English 341: The Nature and Development of the Mystery Novel.'"

Ruby looked puzzled. "The Mystery Novel? How is studying that going to help you be a better editor of *Grace* magazine?"

Smyth stopped in the middle of taking off his parka. "I don't know," he said. "Maybe I won't tell Johnson Pickering what course I'm taking. I'll just tell him I'm enrolled in a BA in English and Journalism."

The Smyths' fourteen-year-old son Michael, who had been standing in the living room, turned and walked away, shaking his head.

Ruby looked thoughtfully at her husband. "You did that on purpose, didn't you?" she challenged. "You have a stubborn streak, Mr. John Smyth. You found a way to obey your board without really submitting to it. No wonder your son is so rebellious. He's following your example."

Smyth didn't say a word, but as he hung his parka in the hall closet, he was grinning. "Stubborn independence is a mark of a good editor," he muttered to himself. "I'm already learning how to be a better editor."

# Chapter 3

*Friday, January 2*

"Getting ready for the spring term at Assiniboine University?" Hosschuk asked.

Detective Alexander Devorkian looked up from the papers he was studying and frowned. He was a tall, distinguished-looking man in a well-tailored suit. "Yes," he said. "I intend to succeed this year."

"We failed the last two years."

Devorkian turned a cold stare on the younger man.

"Do you think studying these files again is going to help?" Hosschuk asked, covering.

"That, among other things. I'm convinced there are answers here somewhere," Devorkian said, gesturing toward rows of file folders stacked neatly on his desk, "and I intend to find them." He smiled. "*We* are going to find them."

Hosschuk sighed. "But we've already been through those files dozens of times."

"And we're going to go through them again and again until we find something. I've gotten permission to block off one day a week to work on this case for the next four months. Sit down."

Sergeant Mike Hosschuk deposited his muscular frame in a chair. "Yes, sir."

Devorkian consulted the papers. "Let's start from the beginning and talk this thing through. Lorraine Malthus, a third-year student at Assiniboine University, Commerce major, average grades."

"She was the short, dark one, wasn't she?" Hosschuk himself was of medium height and blond, unusual for someone of eastern European ancestry.

"Five-foot-two, one hundred twenty pounds, dark hair. Two years ago this spring, on the afternoon of Saturday, April 13, she was found strangled a few feet off the central path leading through the

Assiniboine University endowment lands. The medical examiner concluded she had been killed the previous night, sometime after midnight."

"And not found till the next afternoon ten feet off the main path. She hadn't been moved post mortem, and she was only partially obscured by undergrowth."

"Right. You would think she should have been found earlier." Devorkian shrugged. "But you've never been to university. University students don't get up till noon, especially on weekends."

"And it was an anonymous phone tip."

"From a campus phone, at one-o-three p.m."

"Were we able to determine which campus phone?"

"No. It was one of a number of phones installed for student use in places like the student union building, but the call could not be traced to a specific phone. There had been two previous hang-ups to 911 from campus phones at eleven-twenty-three and twelve-o-one. Not unusual since there are often crank calls from the university, but unusual in that these came in the daytime."

"So we wondered if the killer got impatient waiting for the body to be found and reported it himself, anonymously, after hanging up twice."

"Possibly, but not necessarily. Those woods are used by students for all kinds of clandestine activity—smoking up, drug deals, sex of various kinds. All three calls could have come from someone who didn't want to get involved." Devorkian consulted the papers again. "She was strangled—the bruises from the killer's hands were quite evident on her throat. Her slacks were off and lying beside the body, she was not a virgin, but there was no evidence of recent sexual activity."

"Leading us to think that we might be dealing with a sexually impotent pervert who kills because he is unable to rape."

"Yes. That created a panic. Students were afraid to go into the endowment lands for fear there was a sexual predator lurking there waiting for more victims. The problem with that theory is that a predator usually escalates his activity, but there were no further attacks and we strolled policewomen alone through the woods at all hours of the day and night and he didn't take the bait."

"So we started thinking it wasn't a predator and she was killed by someone she knew. She lived in an apartment, right?"

16

"Yes, four young women in a three-bedroom apartment. The others said they didn't know her well and found her through an ad in the campus newspaper. She didn't eat with them and hardly talked to them."

"Do we believe them? They might have got into a fight over dirty dishes in the sink or something and killed her."

Devorkian shuffled through the file folders and pulled out another one. He skimmed through it. "We considered that possibility and did a thorough search of the apartment. We followed all three of the roommates, none of them is a saint, but we didn't find any evidence linking them to the murder." He shuffled the papers some more. "We even sent in an undercover policewoman to get to know them, but she found nothing."

"She's from Winnipeg, right?" Hosschuk asked, looking through another file. "Yeah, here it is. Grew up without a father…Didn't get along with her mother, a woman named Amber Malthus…and moved out at age seventeen."

"Yes, a real Horatio Alger."

"A what?"

Alexander Devorkian, rare among policemen, had a university education and read widely in his spare time. He was known for making literary allusions that his colleagues did not understand. He was somewhat of a Horatio Alger figure himself, having raised himself by intelligence and hard work from inner-city poverty to middle-class respectability. He sighed and looked at Hosschuk, who had also grown up in inner-city Winnipeg but had not risen as far. "I mean she was ambitious. She was putting herself through university—which is why she was sharing an apartment with three other students."

"I thought she was a party girl."

"She was, but that may have partly been for the money."

"She was tricking?"

"More of a mistress. She dated rich university boys for the presents, and then sold some of the presents for money. At least, that was what one of the boys told us, a young man named…here it is, Damon Massinger. He had an alibi, was out of town that weekend, I think. The others were out of town or had other alibis and weren't talking."

"Massinger wasn't her current boyfriend, right?"

Devorkian leafed through the file folders again and pulled out another one. After perusing it for a few moments, he said, "Right. About halfway through her third year, she stopped going to as many parties. She told some people she had a new boyfriend, but she either didn't tell them the name or they forgot it. He apparently never came to the apartment, and we found no phone number or address among her things."

"The Designated Hitter!"

"Yes, that's what she called him."

"Gross. Or an athlete?"

"Maybe. We checked the campus sports teams and got nowhere. Then some idiot leaked that detail to the press, and any real knowledge about the DH was lost in a welter of speculation and rumor. Everybody we talked to after that had an opinion on who he was, but when you asked, they had heard it from someone who had heard it from someone else."

"Her mother had an alibi too?"

"No, but there was no reason to suspect her. She had no motive. They apparently hadn't talked in months."

"So where did that leave us?"

"Robbery. Her purse was missing, but that may also have been to remove evidence."

"What was she doing in the woods after midnight anyway?"

"We don't know. She may have been walking home from the university to her apartment, which was southeast of the endowment lands, but no one saw her on campus that night. It was a cool night, just a few degrees above freezing, but not raining. She was wearing a warm coat."

"So our investigation got a zero."

"The investigation is not over."

# Chapter 4

## *Sunday, January 4*

"John!"

The voice called across the foyer of Central Grace Evangelical Church, echoing off the dark, varnished woodwork.

John Smyth, buttoning the top button on his parka as he headed for the outside door, stopped and turned around. Ruby and the children stopped as well. A well-conditioned, gray-haired man in a gray suit was coming toward them. He had a warm smile and a quiet demeanor, and, at five-foot-ten, he still towered over the Smyths. He grasped John's hand in a powerful grip.

"Hi, Don," John said. "How are you doing?"

"Fine, John, fine. I understand you are thinking of enrolling at Assiniboine University."

"I just signed up for my first course. How did you know about this? Do they tell all of the professors about every new student?"

"No, no. George Peters told me." Peters was another one of John Smyth's board members.

"Oh."

"Life can be difficult for Christians on university campuses these days. You'll find it a lot different from Grace Bible College."

"Yes, I expect so," John said slowly.

"Maybe you should come around to my office and talk before you start classes. I might be able to help you understand what you are getting yourself into."

John was silent a moment. "Did the board ask you to do this?"

The other man smiled. "Not the board officially. George just suggested that it might be a good idea. He's a little concerned about you, I think."

"Oh."

"When's your first class?"

"Wednesday night."

"Why don't you come around to my office late Wednesday afternoon? It's on the second floor of the Riel Building."

"I don't think I can make it Wednesday afternoon. I have some deadlines, and that is church club night for the kids. Could I come after class on Wednesday night?"

"No, I am not usually on campus in the evening."

"Okay, then. What about Thursday afternoon?"

"Alright." The other man smiled. "I have a class until two-thirty and will be in my office after that until about four-thirty."

"Fine." John smiled. "I'll look forward to it."

Outside, tightening his parka hood around his face, John muttered to Ruby, "Why doesn't anybody think I can do this?"

"I think you can do it."

"You're biased."

They trudged on in silence, with the winter sun sparkling on the snow and a brisk wind nipping at their faces. The Smyths lived four blocks from the church, and John insisted that they walk most Sundays. He reasoned that the children would sit quieter during Sunday school and church if they burned off some energy beforehand, and he claimed to find the walk relaxing. Ruby knew it also saved gas money and it would take just as long to go by car by the time their old gray station wagon had warmed up enough to be drivable.

"Kids club is after supper," Ruby said. "That wouldn't stop you from going to see Professor Henderson in the afternoon."

"I guess you'll have to drive the kids to club this year," John answered. The Smyths did not allow their children to walk alone after dark, although in winter crime wasn't as big a concern as the minus-thirty-five-degree-Celsius temperatures. Every year, half a dozen Manitobans froze to death. Alcohol was a factor in most of these cases, but Manitobans had learned never to treat lightly a climate in which exposed skin could sometimes freeze in less than a minute.

"You're changing the subject."

"I have deadlines," John answered stubbornly. "You can drive the kids, and I will walk to the university."

"That's ten or twelve blocks, not counting the bridge over the river."

"I know how to dress for Winnipeg. I'll be fine."

"But is it safe to walk on the campus at night? Remember the murders that have happened there."

"The victims have all been female students."

"I know, but you're…" Ruby hesitated.

"Short?"

"At night with your parka on, they might make a mistake."

"Maybe that's why the killer waits till spring, so he can tell who he's killing."

# Chapter 5

## *Wednesday, January 7*

His appearance was striking, commanding attention. He had the boyish good looks of a younger Robert Redford, the movie star of a former era, with light brown hair over a tanned face. How did he manage that in January in Winnipeg, Smyth wondered, when Smyth himself was as pale as the winter snow? Perhaps the professor had spent the Christmas holidays on a southern beach. He was of medium height but seemed taller, with a trim waist and muscular shoulders and arms. He was younger than Smyth, in his thirties, but he would probably still look younger—and certainly better—than Smyth did right now when he was in his fifties. Smyth shifted uneasily in his chair. He found he had to slouch to make his feet touch the floor and prevent the edge of the chair from pushing against the back of his legs and cutting off the circulation.

By habit, Smyth had chosen a seat near the front. He had found that in church if he did not sit in a front seat, he could not see over the heads of the taller people in front of him. This would not be a problem here. The floor of the classroom sloped down toward the front, and there were a couple of dozen students in a room that could hold about sixty. Smyth noted that all of them were about twenty, half his age. He wondered about them. He found himself thinking of them as boys and girls rather than the young adults they undoubtedly were.

Sitting by herself on the far side of the room halfway back was a tall, big-boned girl with long, brown hair. A couple of rows in front of her were several Indo-Canadian girls with long black hair, and a couple of rows from them a pair of short, pretty Chinese girls with oval faces and flawless complexions. A couple of chairs from them and one row down was a girl with short, blonde hair, a thin face, and a sharp, beak-like nose. Her mouth was set in a straight line, and her chin was thrust forward defiantly.

Smyth noted that very few students seemed to be sitting together. They were scattered over the room like strangers on a bus who only choose to sit next to another passenger when there are no other seats available. Smyth also wondered about what you could really tell from appearances. The girl with the defiant chin, for instance—did that really indicate her attitude, or was it simply a matter of genetics, a physical feature inherited from her parents?

The professor looked up and smiled. He had even, white teeth. His blue shirt and brownish tie complemented his good looks in an understated way. "Good evening," he said, in a rumbling voice that imitated Alfred Hitchcock from an old show on the rerun channel. He smiled, and his eyes sparkled. "I am Professor Dieter Hemenhof. Welcome to my little class on murder." Now he was sounding like Count Dracula.

The students giggled nervously. A movement to his left caught Smyth's eye. A thin student with longish hair, a sharp nose, piercing black eyes, and a small goatee had come into the room and sat down in one of the front seats near the door. He was dressed in blue jeans and a brown turtleneck sweater and seemed to be in a very serious mood.

Hemenhof smiled in his direction. "Good evening, Mr. Tapinski," he said. "Welcome here."

Now that his attention had been drawn in this direction, Smyth noticed that the students seemed to have segregated themselves, with the females on his left and the males on his right. Behind the newcomer and closer to the center of the room was a good-looking athletic youth over six feet tall. He was sitting beside another youth of almost equal height who nevertheless seemed overshadowed, lacking the first student's finely chiseled features and captivating smile. Out of the corner of his eye, Smyth caught the girls on the other side of the classroom glancing in the tall student's direction.

A couple of rows behind the athlete was an average-looking youth with blond hair and a crooked smile.

Smyth almost missed the student sitting at the back of the room, a black trenchcoat markedly inadequate for a Winnipeg winter encasing his thin body, a lip ring prominent on his face. His hair seemed unnaturally black, and Smyth reflected that he seemed vaguely familiar, as if he had seen him somewhere before, in some other context.

"Why are you here?"

Smyth realized with a start that he had been allowing his mind to wander. He was going to have to get used to being in school again, to paying strict attention to the lectures. It struck him that he was approaching this class like a church convention, where what was happening in the audience was often as important as what was happening on stage. Smyth was an inveterate people watcher. People fascinated him. Sitting in an airport or a restaurant, he would watch the people move past him and wonder about their lives, ask himself questions. Ah, yes, the question. Whenever his children asked that question, when they stopped unexpectedly at a store on the way home from school, for instance, and they asked, "Why are we here?" he would invariably answer, "To love God and serve people." He had said it so often that they had memorized it, and it had become an inside joke in their family. But it would not serve here.

"Motive," the professor was saying. "Motive. Why do people do the things they do? Why do they commit murder? That is what we will talk about next week. Why are you taking a class in murder? That is your first assignment, due on Monday. Drop it off at my office in the Riel Building or e-mail it to me. Write a three-page paper on your motives for taking this class, what you expect to get out of it. Think about the themes that we will be covering in the class, as listed in the course outline. What is mysterious about you?"

Good question, Smyth thought. Why were all these students here? He had not considered the only other student sitting in the front row. She was short, only a little taller than Smyth. She had large breasts, a narrow waist and beautiful legs, crossed over one another at the knee. She smiled up at the professor. She wore high-heeled boots and, using one hand, pulled down on the edge of the very short skirt of her red dress to maintain some semblance of modesty. Funny, Smyth thought. Most of the other students were dressed in parkas, sweaters, and other clothing geared to a Winnipeg winter, and this girl was wearing a party dress. On the other hand, she was probably more comfortable in this dry, overheated classroom than he was. An ankle-length leather coat was thrown over a chair beside her, and an oversized leather bag, a foot and a half square stood upright on the floor at her feet. Her face, framed by shoulder-length blonde hair, was heavily made up, with bright red lipstick, bright blue eye shadow, a heavy coat of cover, and spots of rouge on the cheeks.

"There has not always been a mystery novel. It all began with Edgar Allan Poe," Dieter Hemenhof was saying as he paced across the front of the room. "Or, if you are in Britain, with Sir Arthur Conan Doyle. There are some who say it started earlier than that with Wilkie Collins's novel, *The Woman in White,* but people who say that are wrong…" He stopped suddenly, startled by a deep frown etched on the face of the short, bald, red-bearded man in the front row. "Is something wrong, Mr.…?"

"Smyth. John Smyth."

"An assumed name, I presume?"

The class snickered.

"No, it's…" Smyth stammered.

The professor cut him off. "Is something wrong?"

"No, sir. I was just thinking about what you said."

"Oh. You looked as if you disagreed with what I was saying."

"Well, actually…"

"Actually, what, Mr. Smyth?"

"I was thinking it all began with Cain killing Abel, the first recorded murder in history. That's in Genesis 4, the first book of the Bible."

"I see. And who solved that murder mystery?"

"God did."

Hemenhof looked skeptical.

"God interrogated Cain, asking him where his brother Abel was. Cain denied killing his brother, but God knew he had done it and punished him. But I suppose that wasn't really a mystery because God already knows everything."

"And do you know everything, Mr. Smyth?"

"No, of course not."

"Then perhaps it would be a good idea if you let me get back to teaching this class so you might learn some of the things you don't know?"

"Sure." Smyth shrugged. "But you're the one who started the conversation."

"I don't think the professor likes me."

Ruby, on the other side of the bed, did not look up from her book.

"I said, I'm thinking of murdering my wife."

Ruby did not move.

"In fact, I think I will do it right now."

"Don't be silly. That would leave you alone with the kids, and you can't handle them."

"Why doesn't anybody think I can do anything?"

"What?" Ruby finally put down her book.

John sighed. "I don't think the professor likes me."

"Don't be ridiculous. You sound like the kids on the first day of school. *The teacher doesn't like me, and the other kids don't like me either.* You're just worried you won't do well, that's all. It'll be fine once you get used to it and start making friends."

"No, I really think..." Seeing the skeptical look on Ruby's face, John gave up. "What are you reading that's so much more interesting than I am?"

"*A Morbid Taste for Bones.* It's Volume One of the Chronicles of Brother Cadfael."

"Brother Cadfael?"

"He's a twelfth-century monk in Shrewsbury."

John's eyes glazed over. "History?"

"No, it's a series of medieval murder mysteries written by Ellis Peters."

"Who's he?"

"He's a woman named Edith Pageter."

"What?"

"They're really quite good. Maybe we could read them together."

"You mean I would read them to you, and you would fall asleep."

Ruby smiled. "She's really a good writer. I wouldn't fall asleep like I do when you read me your editorials."

# Chapter 6

## *Thursday, January 8*

He had a feel for the layout now, and it did not take him long to find the right place. He did not even have to ask a janitor for directions as he had the night before. The Riel Building was an eight-story, red brick tower in the northeast corner of the campus. The English Department was on the second floor, and Professor Don Henderson's office was near the south end of the hall on the east side of the building. The door was ajar and swung open when John Smyth knocked on it.

Henderson was sitting behind a large oak desk. Both sides of the room were lined floor to ceiling with neat bookcases, and the corners held filing cabinets. Neat piles of books and papers covered the desk, the tops of the bookcases, parts of the floor and virtually every other horizontal surface in the room. The back wall contained a large window which looked out over parking lot D. Smyth noted that there was a good view of the wooded endowment lands to the east of the parking lot, but there was only a limited glimpse of the Assiniboine River to the north. With his broad powerful shoulders, distinguished gray hair, conservative tie, and cardigan sweater, Henderson resembled somebody's wise old grandfather or trusted uncle.

"Hello, John," he said. "Come on in."

"Hello, Don." Smyth sat in one of the two institutional chairs across from the desk, which he noticed did not look as comfortable as the high-backed executive chair that the professor was sitting on. "Nice office," he said.

"It's functional." The professor shrugged and smiled. "The larger offices with views of the river go to professors whose views are more politically correct."

Smyth, whose own office was smaller and more cluttered than this one, did not respond to that.

"I believe you said that your first class was last night."

"That's right."

"What are you taking?"

Smyth hesitated. "English 341."

The professor frowned for a moment, then brightened. "Dieter's course on the mystery novel? What did you think of it?"

"It was, uh, interesting."

"Professor Hemenhof is a good lecturer. How do you think you are going to do?"

"Well, I haven't been in school for a while, but I did okay at Grace Bible College and..."

"That would be a mistake. Don't think of university as being like Bible college."

"I know the standards are much higher here. I'll have to study more, think more clearly, write better papers."

"Yes, that's true."

"May I ask—did you go to Grace Bible College?"

"No, no. I did all of my training in the public university system, finishing up with a PhD from Cambridge."

"Oh."

"It will be harder for you here, but that is not what I was thinking of. It is not just that the standards are higher here. The standards are different altogether. The values are much different." He seemed thoughtful for a moment. "Things have changed since I started my academic career. As you probably know, Assiniboine University, like many universities in Canada, was started as a church college, but it was taken over by the provincial government in 1952. That founding influence lingered for quite a long while. When I came here, the chairman of the English Department was an evangelical Christian. If I applied for a position in the department now, even with the same credentials, I would be turned down. My Christian views are politically out of favor."

"Are you saying there is a bias in the university against evangelical Christians?"

"Yes, a bias against evangelicals, but also a bias against conservative thinkers and against anyone who doesn't adhere to certain philosophical principles which now dominate university thinking."

"But isn't that discrimination?"

"Of course, but it is nothing you could ever prove. Candidates with the wrong viewpoints are rejected on the pretext that they have inadequate teaching experience, inadequate publication records, and so on."

"I thought universities were supposed to be forums for the free discussion of ideas."

"They are, but these days certain ideas are not welcome—if you do not support evolution or abortion or homosexuality, for instance." The professor paused. "The bias is not uniform—there are pockets where politically incorrect ideas are welcomed—and the discrimination is quite subtle. I am fifty-five and an associate professor. I was promoted from lecturer to assistant professor and then to associate professor by the time I was forty. I have a better publication record than almost any other professor in the department. My job is not in jeopardy since I have tenure, and some students appreciate what I teach, but I will not be promoted to full professor. The problem is that my specialty is seventeenth and eighteenth-century English literature, when many of the writers wrote from a Christian viewpoint. Those writers are out of favor today, and so are books and articles about them. I think I am producing better books and articles now than I did twenty years ago, but I am having increasing difficulty getting them published. On the other hand, Dr. Hemenhof, your current professor, is somewhat antagonistic toward Christianity. He is an adequate researcher and a good lecturer, and at thirty-five he is already in line to become chairman of the English Department. He is also lobbying the Canadian government to fund a Chair of Canadian Crime Writing here at the university, with him being appointed to the position, of course. He'll probably get it. There is another professor in the Humanities Department, a Dr. Kingston. He teaches ancient Greek and Roman literature, and it is rumored that at the end of every course, he hosts a party for the students, at least certain of the students. The parties are what he calls 'historically appropriate.' Ancient Rome was quite licentious, and so are Professor Kingston's parties. The students recline on couches, eat grapes, and drink a lot of wine—and frequently that leads to sexual activity. The technical term is a bacchanalia. The more common term is orgy."

"But isn't that…improper…or illegal or something?"

"Well, it is not illegal for students to have sex with one another. In fact, now it is considered part of the university experience. However, if a professor were to have sexual contact with a student, it would be a violation of professional standards and possibly illegal, a form of professional sexual abuse."

"Is Dr. Kingston having sex with students?"

"I have no idea. And no one is going to ask. It is never stated outright that sex is involved in these parties, and so far there have been no complaints from students. In fact, Dr. Kingston's general approach has won him awards for being an innovative teacher. The complicating factor is that Professor Kingston is homosexual, so if the university were to take action against him for his sexual activities, he would probably go to the human rights tribunal and say that the university was discriminating against him. So the university doesn't dare do anything. That is the kind of thing we are up against. You will find Assiniboine University far different from Grace Bible College. It is difficult to be a Christian here. Immorality is condoned, and morality is ridiculed."

Smyth was thoughtful. "Thank you. I think I understand." But he wondered if Henderson was exaggerating the situation.

# Chapter 7

## Friday, January 9

"It's my lucky day. I get to spend it studying these old files again."
The words were said in a dry monotone, with only a slight hint of
humor.

"The fault, dear Brutus, is not in our stars, but in ourselves."

"What?" Hosschuk looked up perplexed.

The dapper Detective Devorkian explained, "It's a quotation from
Shakespeare's play *Julius Caesar*. It means that this task can't be blamed
on bad luck but on human evil. In other words, blame the bastard who
killed these women."

"Oh." Hosschuk shrugged his shoulders. He didn't particularly like
his boss, the well-dressed, well-educated detective with the superior
intelligence and condescending attitude. But Devorkian *was* intelligent,
he was usually fair, and he was a good police officer. Hosschuk
respected him, and whether he liked him or not was not important.

"What gets me," Hosschuk continued, "is how unhelpful the
university has been in this whole thing."

"You're right. They promised us full cooperation when this started,
but they have managed to be cooperative without being helpful,"
Devorkian said. "You have to understand how universities work. They
want the murder solved, but they see that as our responsibility. Their
responsibility is to protect the good name of the university. They don't
want to scare away students. Every student who decides not to enroll
costs the university thousands of dollars. That's why they insisted that
the university is safe and the murder was an isolated incident."

"Then how did they explain the second murder?"

"Another isolated incident. It was a year later."

"A year later to the day."

"You're right, and that is the subject we will be studying today."
Devorkian reached over and pulled several file folders out of a stack.

He opened the top one. "Astrid Andersson, five-foot-ten, one hundred and fifty-five pounds, a first-year exchange student from St. Paul, Minnesota. Her body was found about twelve-thirty in the afternoon on Sunday, April 13."

"A half-hour earlier than the first one."

"Right, but this time there were no earlier hang-ups from campus pay phones. The finding of the body was called in by two female students who used a cell phone and stayed around until we got there. The medical examiner said the victim had probably been killed just after midnight—just like Lorraine Malthus. The body was two or three feet off a side path, about twenty feet from the central path, near the east or city side of the woods. It was a Sunday, and it had been raining off and on, so there weren't many students out in the woods."

"The rain obliterated footprint evidence, right?"

Devorkian opened another file. "The central path through the woods from the university parking lot D on the west to the parking lot of the supermarket on the east is paved…The side path was a secondary path that led north, connecting to another path that ran along the river bank…It was a gravel path—some of the lesser paths are just bare earth—and there were scuff marks still visible, so we think she was killed on the path and pushed over into the bush."

"But the marks were not clear enough to get footprints?"

"It was gravel, so we probably wouldn't have gotten any even if it hadn't rained."

Hosschuk was looking at a different file. "The medical examiner thinks she was killed there. She was strangled, and again the bruises from the killer's hands were obvious."

"Did forensics find any transfer cells from the killer, on her neck or under her fingernails?"

"Hosschuk checked the file. "Apparently not. If there had been some there, forensics speculated they might have been washed off by the rain."

Devorkian shook his head. "Forensics admits to some limitations? I'm amazed."

Hosschuk continued. "Her dress was hiked up, her shoes were off, she was not a virgin, but she had not had sex recently."

"Just like Lorraine Malthus."

"Here's something different. Her blood alcohol level was point nineteen. She was blotto, possibly passed out drunk."

"Wait." Devorkian pulled down another file and searched through it. After a few minutes, he said, "Lorraine Malthus had had a couple of drinks but was not drunk."

Hosschuk began sorting through the files on the desk, but Devorkian found what he was looking for first. He pulled it toward him with a gesture of triumph without looking at Hosschuk. He leafed through it for a few moments and then held up a report. "According to other students, Astrid Andersson had a drinking problem. It is not uncommon for students to drink to excess, being away from home for the first time. Apparently Ms. Andersson had started drinking at age fourteen back in Minnesota, which was one reason she came here—to make a fresh start."

"Probably came for the Canadian beer. Isn't that what the other girls in her dorm said?"

"Women," Devorkian corrected. "The other *women* in her dorm said she got drunk frequently, about once a week."

"She was old enough to drink legally?"

"Nineteen. She had taken a year off after high school."

"We checked for a Minnesota connection, right?"

"Yes, and found nothing of interest. She comes from a lower middle class family, has one older sister. As far as we know, nobody she knew in Minnesota was at Assiniboine University, or even in Winnipeg."

"Then the murderer was local." Hosschuk said. It was a statement, not a question.

"We thought we could even narrow it down to the campus. She lived on campus and apparently had few reasons to leave."

"Except to drink."

"Apparently she drank mostly in the pubs at the university."

"We checked with her friends, right?" Hosschuk asked, sorting through the files.

"If I remember rightly, the other students in her dorm said she didn't have any close friends, just people she drank with in the pubs, mostly other students with drinking problems."

"Didn't the university do anything about that?"

"The university," Devorkian said pointedly, "tried to tell us that her counseling records were private, but we put some pressure on, and they finally let us see them." Devorkian picked up another file and opened it. After a moment, he said, "She saw a counselor nine times, for depression and her drinking problem. The counselor had recommended AA, but there is no record of her doing anything else other than talking to Ms. Andersson. Apparently, the university did not want that known for fear the family would sue the counselor and the university for not doing more to help her."

"We checked the campus pubs, and bars in the city too, right?"

"Of course." Devorkian reached for another file, then shook off the idea with a waving motion. "No one remembered seeing her that night. We also asked whether there were other nights when her movements were unaccounted for, but since she had no close friends and went to different pubs, and the women in the dorm didn't care, no one knows."

A few moments later, Hosschuk put down another file. "We also checked the two girls who found the body. They had solid alibis for the night before, and there is no evidence they knew the victim."

"Why were they walking down that path in the rain?"

"They decided they wanted to quote 'walk by the river and watch the pattern of the rain' unquote. They evidently considered themselves poets. Besides, it had mostly stopped raining by then."

"Any other ideas?"

"Did she have a purse?"

"You've got that file."

Hoschuk shuffled more papers and read. "The purse was found lying beside the body. It contained her wallet, a small amount of cash, keys, gum, lipstick, assorted make-up, some feminine hygiene products, and a couple of unused condoms. It had been mostly wiped clean of prints."

"Meaning the killer had had time to remove any incriminating evidence, which is why he didn't mind leaving it by the body."

"What gets me is why she was stupid enough to go walking in the woods after midnight when she knew another student had been murdered there."

"She was drunk for one thing. Besides, the first murder had been a year earlier, and the students had stopped worrying about it. Going into those woods has been a tradition since before I was a student. You don't change a tradition like that just because a student was unlucky enough to get killed a year earlier. It was too tempting. Those woods are useful for a lot of things, from romantic walks in the moonlight to smoking weed in the bushes." Devorkian was silent for a while.

"You got any ideas?" Hosschuk asked.

Devorkian angrily pushed the files aside. "Ideas? Sure, but none of them any good. Let's look at the possibilities."

"Okay."

"We thought the motive for Lorraine Malthus's murder might have been robbery because her purse was missing. But you don't take off her slacks and then strangle a woman if you are just trying to rob her."

"Maybe he was just going to try to tie her up with the slacks."

Devorkian scowled. "Anything's possible, but that isn't very likely. In any case, we can probably rule out robbery because Astrid Andersson was not robbed."

"So, we are probably looking at a sexual predator. The fact that the murders happened exactly a year apart suggests some weird logic. The guy is probably psychotic, a nut case."

"Maybe, but have you ever heard of a sexual predator who waits a year between victims?"

"Okay." Hosschuk shrugged. "What other possibilities are there?"

Devorkian sighed. "One other theory is that it was a homeless person, a crackhead, somebody from the city side who wandered into the woods and assaulted random victims. The problem with that theory is that it is too much of a coincidence that a crackhead would do it twice exactly a year apart. On consecutive full moons maybe, but not on the same calendar date."

"It was the end of term, right?" Hosschuk suggested.

"So?"

"Maybe it was an end-of-year graduation rite, a sorority dare or something?"

"There are no sororities at Canadian universities. Besides, murder is a pretty serious consequence for a prank. One prank might go wrong, but not two years in a row at the same time of year. Of course, it could also be a cult or something like that—but, while there are a few small religious groups on campus, we have no evidence that she was connected with any of them."

There was a long pause.

Finally, Devorkian said, "The other alternative is there could be two murderers."

"Two?"

"Yes. Maybe Astrid Andersson had a boyfriend, or there was someone else who wanted to kill her. What better way than to kill her on the anniversary of the previous murder in order to throw us off?"

Hosschuk thought about that. "Yes, it makes sense."

"The only problem with it is that the details of the two murders are so similar that the second murderer must have had inside knowledge of the first murder."

"A cop?"

"Not necessarily. It could be someone who witnessed the first murder, or someone who saw the first body in the woods."

"So we try to find whoever saw the first murder?"

"That will be difficult. Remember the three anonymous calls to 911? That means several people may have seen the first body in the woods, but we don't know who any of them is."

"We don't know if the Andersson girl had a boyfriend, do we?"

"It might not have been a boyfriend. It could have been anyone who knew her. But no, we don't know if she had a boyfriend. She didn't seem to have any close friends, so who would she tell?"

"She might have told her drinking buddies."

"She might have, but they say no. And if she did tell them, they were probably too drunk to remember."

"She didn't say anything to her family?"

Devorkian pulled a file back in front of him and consulted it briefly. "She wasn't a letter writer and didn't phone home all that often. She apparently didn't tell her family much. The 'confidential' information we finally got out of the university indicated that she had failed one of her first-term courses, and was in danger of failing two or three courses in her second term."

"She was flunking out?"

"Probably."

"Does that have any bearing on why she was murdered?"

"I can't see any connection. Can you?"

"I'm tired of this university stuff. Too much failure."

"We are not going to fail," Devorkian insisted.

# Chapter 8

## *Sunday, January 11*

"John!"

A dozen heads turned in her direction. But the woman in the stylish blue velvet dress, the designer high-heeled boots, and the carefully coiffed blonde hair was bearing down on John Smyth. He was standing with Ruby and three of his children in the foyer of Central Grace Evangelical Church, looking around for his oldest son, Michael.

The woman had a clear voice, an energetic manner, and strain lines around her blue eyes. She was slightly older than John, about forty-five, and, of course, somewhat taller.

"John, I hear that you are going back to university."

"Yes, Sheila. I'm taking a course. How did you hear that?"

"Mabel Forchower told me."

Mabel Forchower was another member of the board that oversaw publication of *Grace* magazine."

"Mabel is Charlie's first cousin."

Charlie was Charles Hall, Sheila's husband and senior partner in a prestigious Winnipeg law firm. John sighed. He had never been able to keep track of the intricate connections between various members of the Grace Evangelical churches.

"I am so pleased for this wonderful opportunity for you. You'll love university. It will expand your horizons and give you so much more to write about. And you'll have such a better understanding of things that you won't make any more of those embarrassing mistakes. Our Meghan said going to university was the best thing that had ever happened to her."

John did not know what to say. Sheila Hall was evidently an intelligent and well-meaning woman, but she had a tendency to gush. John was struggling with the suggestion that he was in the habit of making embarrassing mistakes as an editor. He was perplexed that everybody seemed to know his business and people were talking about him. And he certainly didn't know what to say about Meghan.

Fortunately, Mrs. Hall was completely capable of holding up both ends of the conversation without noticing that he wasn't contributing much. "You've enrolled in a BA in English and Journalism, right? I know being editor of the magazine is not a lot of work, but you'll probably still only be taking one course at a time?"

"Uh, right. One course at a time."

"You're taking a course this term, right? What course are you taking?"

John hesitated. "English 341."

The woman frowned. "English 341?"

"Uh, with Professor Hemenhof."

"What's the course called?"

John said in a small voice, "The Nature and Development of the Mystery Novel."

"Oh, Meghan took that course her last…" Sheila faltered.

"Mrs. Hall, I'm sorry. I didn't mean to bring up…"

Sheila took a deep breath and regained her composure. "That's quite all right, John. I know you didn't. We need to accept these things. Meghan is in a better place." She paused. "And she so enjoyed that course. Professor Hemenhof was such an interesting lecturer, she said, and handsome too." She raised her hand, pointed finger waving in the air, as if she were trying to get a teacher's attention. "I know. I have just had a wonderful idea. Meghan took such meticulous lecture notes, probably much better than you will be able to do. She had a new laptop and typed ninety words a minute. Then, when she got home, she would print out her notes and put them in a file folder in her filing cabinet. They are probably still there. I will see if I can find them and lend them to you. It will help you so much to get through. I know you're not the brilliant student that Meghan was. This way, her studies will have purpose. She'll be helping you. Oh, I'm so glad I talked with you, John."

John stammered. "Notes?…Yes, thank you…That would be nice…I mean helpful, very helpful."

He did not say any more as Sheila had fluttered off in the direction of the coat rack, looking for her designer fur coat.

"Don't look so stunned," Ruby admonished. "That was very thoughtful of her."

"I-I didn't quite know what to say about Meghan."

"Yes, it's obviously still very painful for her."

"It would be. And talking to her about mystery novels was like putting fiction side by side with reality. I felt guilty. I hadn't thought about it before, but when you make entertainment out of such a serious subject as murder, it seems almost sacrilegious, as if you are trivializing human life."

"I thought at first you were afraid she would tell Charlie's cousin what course you are taking."

"Yes, I thought about that too. And of course Mabel Forchower would tell the rest of the board. But why doesn't anybody think I can do this?"

# **Chapter 9**

## *Wednesday, January 14*

"Ah, the usual suspects, I see."

This time the accent was that of a British police detective. The class giggled.

Professor Hemenhof pulled a sheaf of papers from his oversized briefcase and continued, "I have marked your first papers about your motivation for taking this class. It was interesting to see the motives that were revealed—and the motives that were hidden." He turned to the short middle-aged man in the front row. "My friend, Mr. Smyth, for instance, gave three reasons for taking this course,"

The little man remained silent.

"What's the matter, Mr. Smyth? Don't you remember the three reasons?"

"Oh, you mean you want me to repeat them?"

"That would be helpful, Mr. Smyth."

"Okay. The first reason relates to general educational goals. I said that I had seen a murder once and that I took this course to think about that and to broaden my understanding of the world. Second, I wanted to explore the theoretical connection between murder and Christian morality. Third, I am an editor, and this course is part of a program I am taking to improve my writing and editing skills."

Hemenhof stared silently at his student for a moment. "Very cogent, Mr. Smyth."

Smyth smiled.

"But you missed the point of this assignment."

Smyth's smile turned into a puzzled frown.

Hemenhof continued. "This was a very precise assignment. It was not a research paper. It was to be a reflection of your personal motives. What you have given me is three perfectly respectable academic reasons for taking this course, but academic reasons are not what really motivates people to take courses—or to commit murder. What really makes you tick, Mr. Smyth?"

The professor handed Smyth his marked paper, then turned to his left. One by one he began calling out names and handing back the papers.

"Tyler Tapinski." This was the thin student with the small goatee sitting near the door. The students were sitting in almost exactly the same places as they had in the first class.

"Don Hamilton." He was the tall, good-looking athlete, with the captivating smile.

"Brendan Mann." He was the slightly shorter, slightly darker, slightly less handsome, slightly less confident boy sitting next to Hamilton.

"Derek Uluchuk." He was the average-looking blond boy behind them.

"David Horcoff." He was the darker-than-life student with the lip ring sitting in the back row.

Hemenhof watched him pensively as he took the paper and walked back up the aisle to his seat. Hemenhof handed out several more papers, then turned to the other side of the room.

"Rachel Chu. Mable Chan." The Chinese students with the flawless complexions.

"Balbinder Singh. Rami Bal. Ranjit Gill." The Indo-Canadian girls.

"Molly Pembroke." The tall, big-boned, brown-haired girl near the back.

Hemenhof smiled. "Ms Borden," he said.

The blonde woman with the pointed nose and chin sat up straighter, her jaw thrust forward defiantly.

"*Betty* Borden," Hemenhof continued. "I could have guessed why you were here without having read your paper." Turning toward the class with a mischievous smile, he explained, "'Betty' is, of course, short for Elizabeth. In another era, she would probably have been nicknamed 'Lizzie.'"

Ms Borden stiffened. There was a moment of silence, then someone snickered.

"A well-known, real-life murder from the past," Hemenhof said. "*Lizzie Borden took an ax and gave her mother forty whacks, and when she saw what she had done, she gave her father forty-one.*"

"Lizzie Borden was acquitted," Ms. Borden pronounced in a surprisingly thin voice.

"Yes, she was," Hemenhof agreed. "But she had to live down suspicion the rest of her life. And apparently that is a battle you are still fighting, and *that* is why you are here. A good answer." He handed Ms. Borden her paper.

Hemenhof brightened. "And last but not least, Pamela Wright."

The girl with the short skirt in the front row tossed her head of blonde hair, but Hemenhof did not give her her paper. "Hers was the only A paper in the class, the only truly honest answer." Holding up the paper, he read, "I want to experience all of life, to love, laugh, sing, dance, and cry. I want to learn from the lives of the other students. I want to read books that will tell me things that I have never known or felt before. I want to learn what it feels like to hate and love and maybe even kill." He paused. "That is a truly honest answer. It is a selfish seeking of pleasure. That is what really motivates human beings."

Hemenhof handed the paper to Ms. Wright, returned to the lectern at the front of the room, and opened his notes. "There are close to a hundred mysteries published in Canada each year, according to statistics from the Crime Writers of Canada, and two or three thousand in the US. That is about two or three percent of the hundred thousand or so new novels published in the US every year. Why are so many crime novels written? Why are so many read? A primary reason is that we want to experience murder by proxy. We want to learn what it feels like to do something we don't dare to do ourselves.

"Why do people commit murder? Arthur Train, in his classic book *Courts, Criminals and the Camorra,* stated that the primary motives for committing murder are money, love, and revenge. Now, as the people who commit murders and the people who invent murders in fictional form do, we can further break down that list into subcategories such as greed, lust, jealousy, envy, fear, anger, hatred, and thrill-seeking. But those motives are not just the motives of people who commit murders. They are emotions every one of us feels, and we read mysteries to live out those emotions we don't dare to act on ourselves."

"Professor, are you suggesting that one of us could commit a murder?" Molly Pembroke asked, unexpectedly interrupting the flow of Hemenhof's rhetoric.

"Precisely," he replied without hesitation. "Look around you. One of you may be a murderer."

*****

The paper was no longer in his hand as he lay in bed beside Ruby that night, but John Smyth could still see it clearly, particularly the blood-red lettering scrawled at the top of the page. He wondered where Hemenhof got a pen that color. He also wondered what he was going to do about it.

"John?"

"Yes."

"Is something wrong?"

"Professor Hemenhof didn't like my paper."

"You're not going to start that 'the teacher doesn't like me' thing again?"

"No. The teacher doesn't like my paper. He gave me a C minus."

"So?"

"So, that's not good enough. I need a B minus average in my core courses to stay in the program."

"It's only the first paper. Maybe you'll do better next time."

"The professor also said that the reason we read mystery books is that we want to experience what it is like to kill someone but we don't have the courage to actually do it ourselves, so we read about somebody else doing it."

"Is that why you read mysteries?"

"I don't think so. But I can't figure out whether Professor Hemenhof is serious."

"What do you mean?"

"The professor says a lot of provocative things, but I haven't figured out yet whether he really means them or he is just saying them to get us to think."

"Oh."

"There is something else. One of the other students is named David Horcoff. He's a thin kid with a lip ring and very black hair, always dresses in black. He seems familiar."

"David Horcoff?"

"Yes. Mean anything to you?"

"It sounds familiar, but I don't know from where. It's getting late. Forget about the class for tonight. Let's just read our book."

John sighed and reached for the book on the night table—*A Morbid Taste for Bones* by Ellis Peters.

# Chapter 10

*Friday, January 16*

"It's the third victim that's confusing," Alexander Devorkian said, pushing himself away from the files on his desk and leaning back in his chair. His conservative blue tie was pulled slightly to one side, marring his otherwise immaculate appearance.

"I didn't think anything ever confused you," Hosschuk said, looking up from the file he was reading. "What's confusing about her?"

"She doesn't fit. We had two murders exactly one year apart. Then, suddenly, a third one occurs just a few days after the second. Read me those details again."

Hosschuk shuffled papers. "The body of Meghan Hall was found at nine-fifteen on the morning of Wednesday, April 16, pushed under some bushes on the north side of the central path through Assiniboine University's endowment lands, about a hundred feet from university parking lot D. She was five foot six, weighed a hundred and twenty-nine pounds, and had shoulder-length blonde hair. Sounds similar to me. A good-looking girl dumped in the endowment lands."

"Woman."

"Girl. Woman. She's still dead."

"How did she die?"

"She was strangled, her shoes were off, and her slacks were lying beside her. Sounds the same."

"Okay, when did she die?"

"The medical examiner said two or three hours before midnight."

"Precisely. She was strangled like the others, but the others were killed after midnight, and she was killed quite a bit earlier, right?"

"That's what the ME said."

"And he also said that, unlike the others, she was killed elsewhere and dumped in the woods later."

"Right," Hosschuk conceded, "but probably dumped a couple of hours after midnight, about the same time as the first two were murdered."

"Okay, but the victim was different too. The first two were party girls. Meghan Hall was a virgin—if you can believe that these days—and a straight A student, and she hadn't been drinking."

"Wasn't there something about that virginity thing?"

Both policemen turned back to the files. "Here it is," Devorkian said after a while. "Meghan Hall had a purity ring that her parents said she always wore around her neck. There's a close-up picture of it in the file here. It wasn't found on her body or in her bedroom at home. In any case, it suggests she is significantly different from the other victims."

"So the killer chooses his victims at random. He doesn't know them, just attacks whoever happens to be wandering through the woods."

"But Meghan wasn't killed in the woods."

"So, he saw an opportunity somewhere else and then dumped her body where the others were."

"A crime of opportunity?"

"Sure."

"Then why arrange the slacks and put the body with the other ones? That speaks of an orderly mind."

"Or a compulsive one."

"Perhaps."

"Besides..." Hosschuk pulled open another file. "People change. Maybe she was becoming a party girl. Maybe she deliberately got rid of the ring. She had a new boyfriend, an unsavory character, and her mother was worried that they might be having sex."

"Yes, skinny kid who always wore black and had a nose ring."

"David Horcoff."

"So what *do* you think?"

"It smacks of a copycat. The MO is different, and the victim is different."

"And that made the boyfriend the prime suspect."

"Absolutely. He admitted they had planned to meet that night." He consulted a file. "At ten o'clock at The Mystery of Chocolate—that's a dessert shop in the business district at the other end of the endowment lands to the university. She had also told her mother that she was going to study at the university and planned to meet Horcoff afterwards."

"They had an argument about it."

"Right. That's something else that's different, by the way. Meghan lived at home with her parents, Charles and Sheila Hall, and two younger sisters. It is a stable, upper middle class family, a straitlaced, church-going family. The father is a prominent lawyer. You can understand why they didn't like Horcoff. He comes from a working class family, and his parents are divorced. He wears black, dyes his hair, and has a nose ring and tattoos. He was arrested twice as a juvenile, for shoplifting and vandalism."

"Sounds like a prize. Why did this Meghan Hall go out with him?"

"That depends on who you ask. Horcoff says they were in love. Meghan's mother says Meghan felt sorry for him."

"If *he* was dead, we would suspect the parents."

"Precisely."

"He still sounds like a good bet to me. What's his alibi?"

"He doesn't have one. He showed up at the dessert place a few minutes after ten…"

"He was late?"

"Yes. He waited there till about eleven-thirty and then left. He was remembered because he was loud and obnoxious, got into an argument with some other customers about them sitting at his favorite table."

"How does he explain that?"

"He said he was upset because Meghan hadn't showed up, but that kind of behavior wasn't unusual for him. He usually had a chip on his shoulder anyway."

"He could have been hyped up because he had just killed Meghan."

"Sure."

"What about her?"

Devorkian consulted some papers. "A friend saw her studying in the library just before nine o'clock. She had an exam the next day. Nobody remembers seeing her after that."

"It still all points to Horcoff. She studies in the library till about nine-thirty, nine-forty, then heads for the dessert shop to meet Horcoff. But Horcoff has other plans. He meets her in the woods for some nooky-nooky, but Miss high-and-mighty lawyer's daughter isn't giving him any, so he kills her and stuffs her under a bush. Then he rushes down to the restaurant to establish his alibi, making a loud enough impression to be remembered. Afterward, he goes back to the woods, moves the body, and arranges it to look like the work of the serial killer, who had killed his second victim just a couple of weeks earlier."

"It makes sense to me."

"So why haven't we arrested him?"

"There's no direct evidence. It started raining about midnight. We couldn't find anywhere else in the woods where the body was lying, and if there was trace evidence on her or her clothes, it was all washed away. There was one toe print in the mud by the sidewalk, but that might have been made by one of the people who found her."

"Who found her?"

Devorkian pulled open another file. "A group of twelve students who were on their way to the university to write an exam. They phoned it in on a cell phone, but not all of them waited for the police to arrive. The ones who left apparently felt their exam was more important, and the ones who stayed probably saw it as a good excuse to get out of it. They didn't all know each other."

"So this one was found earlier. That's another difference."

"But probably not a significant one. On a weekday, students were up early for an exam. On a weekend, they slept in."

"If this was only a few days after the second murder, why weren't we watching the area?"

"The first two murders occurred exactly a year apart. We weren't expecting a third victim till a year later. We were around for the first couple of days, but we decided it was a waste of manpower to stake out the endowment lands."

"Maybe it was an escalation. He killed one girl the first year..."

"Woman."

"Okay, one *woman* the first year and two *women* the second year. So that means he could escalate to three victims this year."

"Yes, and that is why we need to catch him before spring."

# Chapter 11

## Wednesday, January 21

"The eight of them often went on dates together, even though the relationships became a little complicated." Hemenhof paused. "Write that down exactly. For those of you without a clue"—he glanced at the short, dumpy man in the front row—"you can now say that you have one." He paused again. "Write this down too: Rob was dating Laura, and his friend Roger was dating Bev, even though Bev would have preferred Rob."

Hemenhof had the class's full attention. The students were confused, but listening.

"Those are the first two clues for your second assignment. Instead of just reading about other people solving mysteries, this is an opportunity to see if you can solve one yourself. Each week, I am going to give you another clue. The assignment is to put the clues together and then write a short paper explaining who killed whom and how you figured that out from the clues given. If, at the end of the course, you haven't figured it out, write down the parts that you have figured out."

There was a confused silence in the classroom. Betty Borden raised her hand. "How does this relate to the major paper?"

"The major research paper requires extensive reading and analysis and is worth forty percent of your final mark. This assignment is worth ten percent of your final mark. However, any student who can solve the mystery will receive a bonus of ten percent. My cell phone number is on the course handouts, and I am in my office many evenings till midnight. So, if you figure it out, call me or come in to see me and present your case." He paused. "Sound easy? This assignment has been part of this course for five years, and so far only two students have gotten the right answer. However, I am going to give you an opportunity that I did not give students in previous years. I will allow you to work together on this project, and if you can discover the right

49

answer as a group, I will give all of those in the group ten extra marks. This is not a requirement, but I suggest that those who are interested in this idea might meet after class, form a group, or groups, and decide on some ambient location in which to carry on your discussion."

*****

The Mystery of Chocolate sat defiantly in the business district to the east of the university endowment lands, a dingy storefront establishment incongruously staffed by the anorexic, androgynous waifs who make up such a large portion of current university student populations. There, students who couldn't afford a bus pass still found the money for a six-dollar piece of peanut butter chocolate chip cheesecake. Originally launched as a desperate gamble, a hole-in-the-wall offering ridiculously rich desserts, it caught on. Seizing its brief moment of glory, it expanded into the vacant space next door and began offering lunches of bean sprout sandwiches and watercress salads. Word spread further. In time, in the evening, the hordes of dreamy-eyed students in blue jeans and sweatshirts were joined by after-ballet crowds of late middle-agers in suits and evening gowns; at first it was professors and other intellectuals, then media people and the captains of industry. This had been achieved even though the décor had never been improved from uncomfortable metal chairs grouped around inadequately small tables. The menu was scrawled artistically in chalk on an impossibly long blackboard along one wall. And eventually, when it had become very well known indeed, the dessert shop had begun attracting middle and working class couples like John and Ruby Smyth, splurging on a big date.

John Smyth was sitting now across a table from Molly Pembroke and looking at a foot-high mound of cherries, chocolate, and whipped cream the restaurant called black forest cake. He was wishing Ruby were here with him, wondering whether he should take some home for her, and wondering how he had gotten here in the first place. How wasn't technically a mystery. They had walked, along University Avenue around the endowment lands, because the women had been hesitant to walk through the woods after dark or get into John's old gray station wagon.

Smyth thought about that scene at the end of the class. The students, bleary-eyed after the three-hour lecture, had congregated at the front of the room in the space between the lectern and the chair where Smyth had been sitting. Handsome, athletic Don Hamilton had squared his shoulders, turned, and walked back up the aisle and out the door, followed somewhat hesitantly by Brendan Mann. Balbinder Singh, Rachel Chu and their friends, seeing this, had gathered their belongings and walked single-file out the door at the front of the room. Pamela Wright had leaned forward dramatically, pulled an oversize furry hat out of her oversize handbag, and, after several adjustments, settled it on her perfectly coiffed blonde hair. Then she had taken her long leather coat from the chair beside her, pulling back her shoulders and thrusting out her chest as she put it on. Somehow she had managed to make the simple act of putting on her coat look sexually suggestive. However, rather than join the other students, she had picked up her oversize bag and walked out the door.

Professor Hemenhof had stood against the wall by the door, his large briefcase on the floor beside him, watching the students with an amused smile on his face.

John Smyth had felt awkward about taking the initiative with these students who were much younger than he was and might be unwilling to accept him as one of them. "Well," he had begun, "I guess we should form a group to work on the project."

"Right," Derek Uluchuk had answered breezily. "Shall we adjourn to the Ambrosia Club?"

"The pub?" Smyth had said.

"I don't think I want to go to the pub," Molly Pembroke had suggested hesitantly. "It would be, uh, hard to talk there. Maybe we should go somewhere else."

And so it was that the six of them were seated somewhat awkwardly around a table that would have been crowded with four.

"Okay, anybody figured out whodunit yet?" Derek Uluchuk asked.

"It's rather hard to solve it from only two clues," Betty Borden stated.

"Then why are we here?" Molly Pembroke asked.

"We're here because some narrow-minded people insisted on imposing their bourgeois morality on the rest of us when we would rather be relaxing in the Ambrosia Club." Tyler Tapinski said, looking pointedly at Molly, who seemed shocked by this direct challenge.

"I'm here because I need the marks," Smyth said, filling in the awkward silence. "I'm surprised the others didn't come. I thought Pamela Wright was going to join us, but then she left."

"She doesn't need more marks. She got the only A on the first assignment," Molly said bitterly.

"Yes," Smyth said. "I found that surprising. She seems…"

"A mindless twit?" Derek Uluchuk asked.

"I wouldn't have said that," Smyth responded.

"You don't need to," Derek said. "I already said it. It doesn't matter. I've been in classes with her before. She'll do all right. The higher the skirt, the higher the mark. You can't compete with her because she has better legs than you do."

"How do you know? You and Professor Hemenhof have never seen my legs."

"You're pretty funny for an old man," Derek said, chuckling. "But showing your legs is not going to get you anywhere with Professor Hemenhof. With Professor Kingston maybe, but not with Hemenhof."

"Dr. Kingston? What's she teach?" Smyth asked.

"It's a he, but he's gay," Betty Borden put in.

"Oh," Smyth said. "I think I've heard about him."

"You're disgusting," Tyler Tapinski said to Derek. "Professor Hemenhof doesn't live by your crude standards. He has a progressive, scientific mind, and he gives students the marks they deserve."

"All the same, I bet Pamela Wright would have come to this discussion if Don Hamilton had come," Molly said bitterly.

"Who's Don Hamilton?" Smyth asked.

"Tall, good-looking guy," Derek answered. "Plays on the football team."

"And you sit near him so you can think the girls are looking at you," Betty Borden said pointedly.

"Me?" Derek asked. "I just like to be with people. That's why I joined this group. I don't think we're going to solve Hemenhof's puzzle. I just like to be with people."

Smyth thought again about why he was there and why the others were there—buoyant Derek Uluchuk, serious-minded Tyler Tapinski, big-boned Molly Pembroke and pointy-faced Betty Borden, whose looks would never earn them extra marks, and sullen David Horcoff, who was the only one in the group who had not said a word.

*****

"You're late coming home." Ruby was already in bed, but awake, reading.

"I went out for coffee with some of the other students after class."

"See, I told you the other kids would like you if you gave them a chance."

"One of them called me an old man."

"Remember what you tell the kids: Sticks and stones will break your bones, but don't pay attention to people calling you names."

"It was the professor's idea."

"For them to call you names?"

"No, for us to go out for coffee. He gave us this project, a kind of mystery puzzle which we can work on together. The assignment's worth ten marks, but if we solve it, we will get ten extra marks."

"See, you have a chance to improve your marks. I told you things would get better. Where did you go for coffee?"

"Um." John mumbled.

"Where?"

"Um, The Mystery of Chocolate."

"We can't afford to have you go there every week."

"It was either there or the campus pub."

"We can't afford to have you go there either. You'd be fired."

"I could always say it was Johnson Pickering's idea."

"I don't think so, and anyway you changed the subject."

"From what?"

"From the fact that you went to The Mystery of Chocolate, leaving me home alone with the kids."

"I brought you some black forest cake."

"Where is it?"

"Downstairs in the fridge."

"Go get it."

# Chapter 12

*Friday, January 23*

"Can I ask your opinion on something?" Hosschuk asked.

"Of course," Devorkian answered.

"I've been reading through this file," Hosschuk continued. "About that theory by the university guy."

"What theory?"

A couple of weeks after Lorraine Malthus was killed, one of the professors"—he consulted the file—"Professor Don Henderson of the English Department, came to the police to tell us about a Thomas Robert Malthus, who had written a book called *An Essay on the Principle of Population*."

"The Malthusian theory."

"I guess so."

"I don't remember this."

"No, I think he spoke to…here it is…Detective Harder."

"What did he say?"

"Who?"

"This professor."

"Which one?"

"I don't care. What's in the file?"

"Well, this Professor Henderson came to tell us about this Thomas Malthus's theory."

"Malthus said that human population will always keep increasing to a point where it is no longer sustainable and some people die of starvation and poverty."

"You know about it?"

"Yes, I studied it in university. It's quite a well-known theory." Devorkian looked at Hosschuk and shrugged. "Well-known in university circles."

"Okay. Well this Professor Henderson said that since Malthus talked about there being surplus population and people dying, and since the first victim's name was Lorraine Malthus, maybe there was some connection. His idea was that some wacko had studied this Malthus's theory, and then killed Lorraine Malthus because she had the same name and so she was part of the surplus population or something."

"That would mean that the killer knew her name."

"Yeah. So what do you think?"

"It's possible. Does the file say if Harder followed up on it?"

"No. That's about all there is."

Devorkian considered. "I'm not sure it helps us much in trying to identify the murderer. If true, it just means he is associated with the university somehow, which we already assume. It might provide a motive for the first murder, but how does it relate to the other two murders?"

"I don't know. You said this Malthus guy talked about the population growing, so maybe the wacko thinks the number of murders should grow too."

Devorkian was frowning. "That ties in with Malthus's theory alright. He talked about recurring crises. The population grows to the point that it can no longer be sustained, a crisis occurs, and many people die off due to famine or drought. Then the population grows again, maybe even larger due to improvements in technology, until a new limit is reached, and there is another mass die-off."

"Sounds depressing."

"It is a depressing theory, alright. It's not accepted by a lot of scholars."

"Do you think there is anything in it?"

"Maybe. The number of students at the university grows each year, a crisis comes—perhaps final exams or the end of term—and the killer feels he has to resolve the tension by killing off the surplus population."

"So, he killed one person the first year and two the second year. Does that mean he might kill more this year?"

"It's a good possibility. That would explain why he only kills once a year, but he would have to be one very psychologically disturbed individual."

"He should be pretty easy to spot then."

"Not necessarily. Universities are a breeding ground for eccentric personalities. And psychopaths are often good at hiding their true natures."

"So how could we follow up?"

"One way might be to try to figure out who had studied Malthus's theory. That would not be easy because there probably aren't any courses just on Malthus. His theory is not that important. It would just be mentioned in passing in a variety of courses. Of course, if the killer became obsessed with Malthus, he might have written a paper on him. Finding out which students might have written such a paper would require a lot of work and cooperation from the university."

"Do you want me to do it?"

"No, better leave that to me. I have a better understanding of how universities work." Devorkian paused. "There is one other possibility."

"What?"

"What do we know about this Don Henderson?"

"Psychotic killers often try to get involved in the investigation, you mean?"

"That's it. See what you can dig up on him."

# Chapter 13
## Wednesday, January 28

"While they didn't invent it, it seems to be pretty clear that the English perfected the murder mystery," Professor Hemenhof was saying. "Although there are exceptions, British mysteries have mostly focused on the mental puzzle in which the hero—and the reader—tries to put the clues together and figure out whodunit. The terms 'mystery' and 'whodunit' indicate this, that the focus is on the search for truth even more than the search for justice. Another term for such novels is 'cozy', based on the model of a cozy upper class British household, in which someone has been murdered and the suspects are limited to the small number of people present in the house.

"The heroes of such novels are therefore people of great mental ability. This pattern was set with Arthur Conan Doyle's Sherlock Holmes, who excelled in deductive logic." Here Hemenhof paused, raised one finger in the air and shouted, "It's elementary, my dear Watson!" He then went on in a normal tone of voice, "The pattern continued through Agatha Christie's Miss Marple and Hercule Poirot, with his reliance on his 'little grey cells.' It has continued more recently with Colin Dexter's Inspector Morse and P.D. James's Adam Dalgliesh. Dalgliesh writes intellectual poetry!

"Of course, this seems appropriate for a nation that has produced Cambridge and Oxford Universities, great writers such as William Shakespeare and John Milton, and great thinkers from John Locke to Stephen Hawking."

Hemenhof strode purposefully around the room as he spoke, varying the volume and texture of his voice and using hand gestures. "The characters in many of the early English mysteries spoke disparagingly of American 'potboilers,'" he continued. "The English writers of those books had noticed a significant difference. While the English were writing 'mysteries,' Americans were writing things called 'thrillers' and 'suspense novels.' In these novels, tracking down the killer did not require exceptional intelligence but rather exceptional courage and strength. The quintessential American hero was a tough-talking detective such as Dashiell Hammet's Sam Spade, Raymond Chandler's Philip Marlowe, or Ross Macdonald's Lew Archer, who seemingly couldn't get through a book—and sometimes a chapter—without pulling out a gun and shooting at someone or beating someone up. These heroes did not try to deduce the truth from someone's words and other clues as Sherlock Holmes would have done. Rather, they would grab the witness by the lapels, ram him against a wall, and threaten to tear him limb from limb unless he told them what they wanted to know. Hercule Poirot was too much of a sissy to solve an American murder, and Miss Marple would most likely end up as a victim, not the heroine."

"Americans are stupid and violent!" Tyler Tapinski had unexpectedly and emphatically interrupted the flow of the lecture.

Hemenhof turned on him. "Mr. Tapinski, that's enough of your left-wing propaganda. This is an academic lecture hall. We do not resort to name-calling or make disparaging remarks about other nations." Returning to the lectern, he continued, "Now back to my lecture. The heroes of American crime novels are like this because Americans are stupid and violent."

The class laughed.

"Seriously, the United States is a more violent society than British society is, and that is reflected in the type of mystery novels that are written."

"What are Canadian mysteries like?" Betty Borden asked.

"I'm coming to that," Hemenhof said. "The quintessential Canadian hero is Howard Engel's Benny Cooperman. Compared to Sherlock Holmes and Hercule Poirot, he is an intellectual dwarf. He is a high school graduate and not nearly as intelligent as his university professor girlfriend, Anna Abraham." Here Hemenhof puffed up his chest and struck a cheesy, arrogant pose. "He is also not a tough, American-style detective. He doesn't carry a gun. He is of below average height and is not particularly powerful. He has been beaten up occasionally, but he has never actually hurt anyone else. He certainly isn't going to intimidate a witness into telling him what he needs to know. Not all Canadian heroes are this powerless—many are working policemen—but none are exceptionally intelligent or exceptionally tough and powerful."

"So how do Canadian heroes solve their cases then?" Betty asked.

"In typical Canadian fashion," Hemenhof answered. "By dogged persistence and quiet, unassuming hard work, mixed in with a good dose of luck. In short, Canadian heroes muddle through. Remember Inspector Japp, the foolish police inspector in the Hercule Poirot novels who runs all over the place looking for clues? In a Canadian novel, Inspector Japp would be the hero."

Hemenhof paused, noticing the frown on the face of the short, dumpy man in the front seat. "What's the matter, Mr. Smyth? Do you disagree?"

"No, I was thinking that what you said makes sense. And I was realizing that there is a close parallel among church leaders. The British church has produced great thinkers and theologians such as C.S. Lewis, G.K. Chesterton, John Stott, and J.I. Packer. In contrast, the outstanding Christian leaders in the United States are more action-oriented people such as Billy Sunday, Martin Luther King, John Wimber, and Benny Hinn, people who talk about 'muscular Christianity,' 'power evangelism,' and 'the health and wealth gospel.'"

"And in Canada?"

"I don't think we have many great church leaders in Canada, just a lot of hard-working Christians."

"I don't think there are a lot of very intelligent church leaders in Canada either. And I don't think hard work alone is going to get you through this course."

# Chapter 14
## Friday, January 30

"Did you make any progress on that Malthus theory?"

Devorkian smiled. "You first. What did you find out about Don Henderson?"

Hosschuk smiled his boyish grin and opened a file. "He's an associate professor in the English department, I guess pretty good at his job. He's from Ontario originally and went to the University of Toronto and Cambridge University. He has been teaching at Assiniboine University for twenty-five years. He's fifty-five, but stays in shape—he's five-foot-ten and works out at the campus gym. Outside of work, he is apparently involved in a church called Central Grace Evangelical Church…"

Devorkian rolled his eyes.

"He's a leader…" Hosschuk checked his notes. "Called an elder, whatever that is. He doesn't seem to have any other community involvements. He has no criminal record, not even speeding tickets, as far as I can tell. He was married and has two kids, Ken and Leah, who are studying at universities in Ontario. Want the details?"

"No. What do you mean 'was married'?"

"He was married for twenty-seven years to a woman named Adrienne Parr. She died of cancer almost three years ago, on April 3."

"A year before the first murder. That's interesting."

"Yeah. I thought so."

"Interesting, but it doesn't prove anything. Did you find any connection between him and any of the victims?"

"No."

"Wait." Devorkian began rummaging through the files on his desk, finally pulling out one and leafing through it for a few minutes. "Here it is. Meghan Hall was also a member of Central Grace Evangelical Church."

"I don't think any of the other victims went to church, and we didn't find any connection between Meghan and the other victims."

"I know, but did any of them have some other connection with Don Henderson? What we're going to have to do is track all of the courses that all of the victims took."

"Haven't we done that?"

"There is probably some information in the files. I remember we did some work on it, but I don't think we got very far."

"That reminds me. What did you get on the Malthus thing?"

Devorkian blew out his breath loudly. "There are two ways we could get at that information. The university files don't list the titles of student papers, except for graduate students' dissertations. That kind of information is kept by the professors. So one thing we could do is ask all the professors to check their records and see if any students wrote a paper on Malthus or showed a special interest in Malthus. The other way of approaching it would be to check the university library records and see who checked out books on Malthus and his theory."

"So the information is there, and we should be able to get it, right?"

"Wrong. The university says that allowing the police to check the library and research records of students would violate the principles of academic freedom that are the foundation of the university system. It would set a precedent of allowing the state to make unwarranted intrusions into the private lives and thoughts of students, most, and perhaps all, of whom are innocent of this crime."

"You're quoting right?"

"Right, direct from Dr. Julian Randolph, academic vice-president. The university won't give us that information without a court order."

"So, get a court order."

"On the basis of what? Some professor's mention of a 200-year-old theory which might have absolutely no relevance to these murders?"

"I thought the university promised us full cooperation in solving these murders."

"Right. As I said before, they promised us full cooperation but have managed to be cooperative without being helpful," Devorkian said. "They don't want to scare away students, since the more students the university attracts, the more funding and prestige it gets. Therefore, while the university wants us to solve the murders, its primary goal is to protect the academic freedom and the good name of the university. They don't want our investigation to disrupt the tranquil, refined atmosphere on campus that is conducive to study and learning."

"The campus police haven't been very helpful either, but at least they didn't get in our way. That surprised me, too. I figured they would claim it was their jurisdiction."

"Again you have to understand campus politics. Two years ago, in some budget cuts, the campus security force was gutted. They only have nine officers left, plus some civilians. They basically handle parking, lost and found, and night watchman duties. Chief Danbury is trying to make the point that he doesn't have enough officers to adequately protect the campus. It's a ploy to get his budget increased. That's also why he announced that he does not patrol the endowment lands and that that is our responsibility."

"I thought it was because the woods are dark and scary and he is afraid to go there."

"That and the fact that murder is way out of his league."

# Chapter 15
## Wednesday, February 4

"Curiosity killed the cat." Professor Hemenhof paused, looking at the confused faces of his students. At least, he had their attention. "Curiosity," he continued. "The human being is a curious animal. He or she wants to know things. And that is why people read mystery novels—to find out whodunit, and why. It is similar to the motive people have for reading other novels. People are interested in people, and if the writer is good, readers become interested in the characters in books. People then read the novels to the end to find out what will happen to the characters. The same motive operates to some extent in mysteries. People read them to find out whodunit, but also to find out what will happen to the central character and to the other characters in the book, not just the murderer and the victim, but also the lesser characters, the red herrings, the people in the subplots.

"Now a strange thing happens to many successful mystery writers. They begin to develop the delusion that they are real novelists. They start to think that readers are so fascinated by their hero—who is usually based on the author—that they will read a whole novel just to find out what is going on in the life of this central character. This is a mistake, because few individuals are interesting enough on their own to maintain readers' interest over a long series of books. It is also a mistake because what distinguishes a good mystery writer is the handling of the intricacies of plot and only secondarily the depiction of character. Agatha Christie was the most successful of all mystery writers, and yet her characters were often described as 'cardboardy,' interchangeable stock characters such as the butler, the maid, or the younger brother. Mystery writers should never forget that the most important character in their books is the mystery. That is why people read mystery novels, what they are looking for. Hercule Poirot's indiosyncracies may be interesting, but they are not nearly as interesting as the mystery plot, and they are best doled out in small doses, a few snippets in each book. Leaving some things mysterious will keep readers coming back to read the next book."

*****

"Harry had a crush on Mary." Molly Pembroke dumped her backpack down on the floor in frustration. "What kind of clue is that?"

Betty Borden sniffed. "This mystery sounds more like a romantic comedy."

"That's what my love life is," Derek said, "a romantic comedy."

"No doubt," Betty sniffed. "You're probably just jealous because some of the people in the clues have dates and you don't."

Derek scowled in mock indignation.

"Remember the clues from last week," Betty said, consulting her notes. "Rob's sister, Mary, had dated Larry and Harry but decided she liked Larry best. And Larry was older than his brother and usually beat him at everything, but his brother wasn't like him at all. Maybe these clues will make sense if we put them all together."

"I doubt it," Molly said bitterly. "No wonder none of his students ever figure out the mystery."

"That's not true," John Smyth said. "Professor Hemenhof said that in five years, two students have figured out the solution."

They were gathered at The Mystery of Chocolate again, the same group as last time, except that Brendan Mann had joined them and Tyler Tapinski was absent.

"I have an idea," Betty Borden said. "Maybe we should track down the two students who found the solution and ask them."

"That would be cheating," Molly Pembroke responded.

"No, it wouldn't," Betty insisted. "You've got to get rid of your farm girl morality or you are never going to make it in the city. We would only be questioning a witness just like they do in mystery novels."

"But how would we find them?" Molly asked. "We can't get student records like the police can or search Professor Hemenhof's office. It would probably be harder to find those two students than it would be to use the clues to solve the mystery."

"Not necessarily," Betty said. "Does anybody here know anybody who took the course before? Even if they didn't figure it out, they might be able to tell us who did." She paused, seeing the troubled look on John Smyth's face. "Mr. Smyth, do you know someone who took the course before?"

"Not exactly. I, uh, knew someone. Well, I didn't really know her. She went to my church, but she, uh, died. Her mother said she would lend me her notes."

"What do you mean she died?"

"She was one of the young women murdered in the endowment lands…"

There was a crash as David Horcoff's chair bounced on the floor. He had stood up abruptly and was heading for the door, leaving a piece of black licorice layer cake half-finished on the table."

"What's with him?" Betty asked.

"What difference does it make?" Brendan Mann put in. "He wasn't contributing to the discussion anyway."

"So? You weren't here last week," Molly charged. "If we get the solution, do you think you deserve to get the same bonus marks as the rest of us?" She paused. "I thought you hung around with Don Hamilton. Why didn't he come?"

"He said he had something to do," Brendan answered sullenly.

"He's probably doing Pamela Wright," Betty said.

"Do you think he might come next week?" Molly persisted.

"I don't know."

"It seems to me," Smyth said, "that anyone who comes should share the credit if we solve the mystery. Who knows? Somebody might show up just the last week but provide the final clue or the final suggestion that we need to solve it."

# Chapter 16

*Friday, February 6*

"I've been thinking," Hosschuk said.

"Good. That's what they're paying you for."

Hosschuk ignored Devorkian's put-down. "The first victim, Lorraine Malthus, said that she called her new boyfriend the Designated Hitter."

"So? We wondered if that meant she was going out with a jock, but we didn't find any evidence she even knew any athletes. She spent her time in the pub."

"The short form for Designated Hitter is DH. Don Henderson's initials are DH."

Devorkian considered. "That might be significant or it might not." He paused. "David Horcoff's initials are also DH."

"Oh." Hosschuk sank down in his chair. "Well, it was a thought." He paused. "I guess that's all we've got left, thinking."

Devorkian smiled. "We've been through all the files. Thinking would help."

"But that's just it. We've been through all the files, and we haven't found anything new. What else can we do?"

"We can go back and interview all of the witnesses again."

"All of them?"

"What else do we have to do?'

"A lot of things far more productive than that, like working on cases we can solve. We haven't got a prayer on this one."

"A prayer?" Devorkian's views on such things were well known. "I don't believe in divine intervention."

"Why not? We need all the help we can get."

Devorkian looked intently at Hosschuk. "Are you talking about John Smyth?"

"I wasn't thinking of him, but he did help us out with that one case."

Devorkian straightened his shoulders. "Mr. Smyth," he lectured, "happened to be in the right place at the right time and came across some evidence." He paused. "And, he was astute enough to recognize it as evidence. I'll grant him that. But he's not God, God doesn't reveal secrets to him, and it's unlikely that lightning is going to strike twice in the same place."

"Lightning strikes the same tall buildings all the time."

"'Tall' hardly suits Mr. Smyth."

They both laughed.

"Look," Devorkian continued. "These murders took place near the university. They're almost certainly connected to the university, and a university is not a place John Smyth is likely to be around. He hangs around churches and neighborhoods, and that's where he found the clues last time. He doesn't move in the right circles for this case. He didn't strike me as very polished or intellectual."

# Chapter 17

## *Sunday, February 8*

"I'm very sorry, John."

"Sorry about what, Sheila?"

"That I didn't get Meghan's notes to you earlier. The term is almost half over. I hope it hasn't been too overwhelming."

"I'm managing to muddle through."

"Good. As I said, I'm sorry it took so long. Meghan had her copy of the notes with her that night…We never got her things back from the police. The police also took her computer, but they gave us a CD with all of her files on it. So I had to print out new copies of all of them."

"Sheila, I'm sorry you had to go to all that trouble."

"It's alight, John. I was glad to do it. Well, things should be fine now. Here they are. There are copies of the lecture notes, notes on her readings, two assignments, and a file called 'clues,' whatever that means. I hope this will help."

"Thank you. Sheila." Smyth looked down at the four-inch stack of paper that she had handed him, neatly organized in file folders. "I don't know what to say."

"Just do your best to pass the course, John. That's all the thanks I need. Meghan never got a chance to write the exam, but God must have had a purpose for her compiling all these notes. Maybe they were meant for you."

"Thank you, Sheila. God does work in mysterious ways." He paused. "Uh, Sheila…have the police made any progress in finding out what happened to Meghan?"

"No, they haven't," Sheila said sadly. "Just after she died, I think they suspected that boy she had been hanging around with. I was so upset with her. I don't know why she insisted on seeing him. They had nothing in common, and he was such a dishonest, evil boy. The police asked a lot of questions about him, but they never arrested him. I guess they just didn't have enough evidence. The police don't tell us very much. I don't know if we will ever find out what happened."

"I'm very sorry, Sheila. I hope you do find out. God sometimes gives us answers when we least expect them."

# Chapter 18

*Wednesday, February 11*

"Are you going to be safe, John? It's already minus thirty."

"I'll be fine, Ruby. I've got my long underwear, my sweater, my parka, and my heavy mitts. It's only about a mile to the campus."

"It had worked so well, with you taking our kids and the Manuel kids to club on the way to class and the Manuels bringing them home. Tonight wasn't a good time for the Manuels to all get the flu."

"It's February. Everybody in Winnipeg gets sick in the winter. If you're going to take Louisa's place helping with the clubs, you'd better get into the church. Don't worry about me. I don't mind walking from here."

"But all the way there and back again is a long way…You aren't going to that coffee thing again tonight, are you?"

"I was planning on it." John paused. "If you're worried about it, why don't you drive down and meet us at The Mystery of Chocolate around ten-fifteen?"

"What about the kids?"

"You can have them in bed before you leave, and Michael will be home from youth group by ten. He can babysit, and since he won't have any advance warning, he won't have had time to come up with anything devious. We'll be home just after eleven anyway."

"But won't I be in the way of your class discussion?"

"It's not an official class. We just get together to talk about an assignment. It's quite informal. You might enjoy it."

"Okay, but don't think this gets you off the hook for Valentine's Day." Ruby smiled. "But I suppose it can't be any worse than those sad-looking flowers you bought me last year."

John grinned. "I explained that. The car wasn't warmed up enough yet when I picked them up. In Winnipeg in February, you're lucky to get any kind of flowers at all."

He trudged down the street. His toque was pulled low on his forehead, and his wool scarf was stretched across the lower half of his face, leaving only a small rectangle around his eyes exposed to the cold. Halfway down the block, he had to step awkwardly out of the beaten path on the sidewalk to get past another similarly clothed individual walking the other way. Idly, he wondered whether he might know the person he had just passed. Experienced Winnipeggers, except for the most fashion-conscious teenagers, dress sensibly for the weather. In winter, even when the sun is glinting off the white snow, it is possible to pass your best friend and not recognize him. One heavily bundled body looks much like another.

Smyth trudged on, gasping for breath now, his lungs burning from the cold. Seasoned Winnipeggers adjust to the cold and by mid-winter find any temperature down to minus twenty Celsius quite comfortable. Below twenty, the cold becomes uncomfortable, and below thirty, breathing becomes difficult. Still Smyth did not mind. He reflected that there were not many things that challenged the manhood of a sedentary editor, but braving a Winnipeg winter was one of them. Not that the life of an editor was easy. He could be quite fearless in publishing articles that challenged the status quo, and he put his job on the line in virtually every issue of the magazine. Raising four kids was also an adventure. But they did not get the adrenaline flowing like the physical challenge he was facing now. He gasped for breath like a climber nearing the top of Mount Everest.

*****

"Good mystery writers carefully work out their plots before they write their books. Lazy writers do not." Professor Hemenhof paused, using the silence to recapture his students' attention. "How many times," he went on, "have you read a mystery in which the author presented several possible suspects and then at the end of the book seemed to choose one of the suspects at random to be the killer, when from the evidence it could equally have been any one of them? That is not playing fair with the reader, and it is a result of the writer being too lazy to think through his plot beforehand. A good mystery writer—and I am talking about classic mystery stories here, British cozies, not

American suspense novels—a good mystery writer will start writing from the end. That is, he will start with the basic plot of A killed B for reason C. That story will have integrity and cohesion. Then he will add in red herrings, subplots and cross-plots, other possible suspects with other possible motives, but in the end these red herrings lack substance, they don't lead to the solution. They should remain subplots.

"The best mysteries are those in which the writer reveals all of the clues but mixes them in so well with red herrings that when the book is over, the reader says, 'I should have gotten it, I had all the clues, but I missed it.' At least, most readers will say that, because if the writer is giving a fair chance to the reader, then some readers will figure it out. The point is that the murderer should be the only suspect who would have killed that particular victim in that particular way at that particular time. That is, the solution to the murder should be consistent not only with the revealed facts or clues but also with the characters of the suspects.

"Remember the famous line, 'The butler did it'? That is because the author will often choose the least likely suspect, the almost invisible person in the background, as the murderer. That makes sense because part of the game is for the writer to fool the reader. It doesn't work as well now, because the butler is the first person experienced mystery readers suspect. We all now look for the least likely suspect, so writers now sometimes cross us up by choosing the most likely suspect."

One of the students giggled, and most looked confused.

Hemenhof went on. "While trying to fool the reader, the writer must still be fair. A recent book by one of the English masters—I won't give away the solution by telling you which one—stressed all the way through the strength required to strangle the young victim face on. Then the author revealed that the killer was a fifty-year-old secretary. The author also revealed the key clue *after* the identity of the murderer was revealed. Not fair. The best mysteries reveal all of the clues without revealing the murderer—until the end. Inferior writers—or good writers not at their best—will either hold back some of the clues or will reveal the clues so clumsily and blatantly that they reveal the mystery too soon."

"By that definition, how many mysteries are good mysteries?" Betty Borden asked.

Hemenhof smiled. "Not very many. What I am talking about is very hard to do. That is what separates the great writers from the average ones." He paused, as if to recollect where he was in his notes. "What I am also talking about is consistency, consistency between plot and character, and that does not just apply to the solution of a mystery but to all fiction writing. For instance, many mysteries feature amateur detectives, people who would not normally be involved in solving crimes. In that case, they must act like amateurs. Agatha Christie's Miss Marple is a good example. She is an old lady from a small town. She solves crimes by thinking and comparing the suspects to people she has known in her village and asking how certain people act. Then she tells the police whom to arrest. That makes sense. A recent Canadian mystery, on the other hand, features a middle-aged woman, a total amateur, who picks up a gun and goes chasing after villains down dark alleys. Who does she think she is? Rambo? The central figure in most of Ross Macdonald's mysteries is Lew Archer, a hardboiled detective. But in one of his early books, *The Three Roads,* he has an amateur sleuth who keeps talking about 'this case' as if he has been involved with a lot of cases. That was a sloppy mistake by a usually very good writer."

*****

On the way over, they had a debate about whether The Mystery of Chocolate would be empty tonight as people stayed home to keep warm or packed out as people sought refuge from the cold. "Like birds eating suet in winter," Molly Pembroke suggested, revealing her farm girl background. It turned out to be the latter. Still they managed to find a table near the back and scrounge enough loose chairs for all seven of them—John Smyth, Molly Pembroke, Betty Borden, Derek Uluchuk, Brendan Mann, Tyler Tapinski, and David Horcoff. Smyth even found an eighth chair, pulled it over beside him, and dumped his battered briefcase and parka onto it. He was sitting beside Tyler Tapinski, with Molly Pembroke on the other side of the eighth chair. Molly had a puzzled frown on her face.

"Mary and Alice often went to the ballet together and were out the night Laura was killed," Betty groused. "Who cares? What does that have to do with a murder mystery? Does anybody have any clue what this stupid mystery is all about?"

Her comment was answered by a chorus of shrugs.

"I don't even get the lectures," Derek said. "All that stuff about characters being in character. How can a character be out of character?"

"I think it makes perfect sense," Smyth replied. "Not just in mystery novels but also in life, people act in keeping with their characters. Jesus said that you don't get grapes from thornbushes, that good people do good because of the good in their hearts and evil people do evil because of the evil in their hearts."

Tyler Tapinski grimaced. "This isn't a religion course."

"No, but it is a course that deals with morality because murder is immoral."

"It's a literature course," Tyler insisted. "It's about the scientific study of literature. Morality has nothing to do with it. Why do you Christian fanatics keep trying to force your religion on everybody else?"

"Hey, go easy on the old man," Derek put in. "He can't help it if he was raised differently from you. Not everyone has Marxist parents."

"My father was a union leader," Tyler answered, "but that's not why I'm a Marxist. I am a Marxist because Marxism makes sense. It fits the facts. It explains why things are the way they are in the world."

"That's strange," Smyth said quietly. "I would say the same thing about Christianity. It's what helps me make sense out of life. Christianity fits reality. You have to admit it fits in pretty well with Professor Hemenhof's scientific analysis of mystery novels."

"I don't have to admit that," Tyler retorted. "It's not true. It's—"

Smyth abruptly stood up. Tyler flinched as if he thought Smyth was about to hit him.

"Sorry I'm late," Ruby said brightly. "Is the discussion going well?"

There was an awkward silence.

"Not particularly," Derek answered.

Smyth said, "This is my wife Ruby. This is Tyler Tapinski, Derek Uluchuk, Brendan Mann, David Horcoff, Betty Borden, and Molly Pembroke."

Ruby shook hands with each one, stopping at David Horcoff. "Hello, David," she said. "How are you?"

David nodded and shook hands silently.

A puzzled look hardened on John Smyth's face.

"Good move," Tyler said. "If you're losing a debate, bring in reinforcements."

Everyone laughed.

"Can I get you a piece of cherry chocolate cheesecake?" Smyth asked Ruby.

*****

"Well, what did you think?"

"It was very interesting," Ruby said. "The students seem nice, and the discussion was interesting."

"Do you really think so? And have you figured out the mystery?"

"No, but I would say that the names in the clues are significant."

"Speaking of significant," John said, "it almost seemed as if you knew David Horcoff."

"Of course. Don't you know who he is?"

"No,' John said. "He's a student."

"When you asked me about David a few weeks ago, I didn't remember his name, but I recognized him as soon as I saw him. He was going out with Meghan Hall. She brought him to church a couple of times. Don't you remember?"

"Not really. I mean I didn't recognize him." He paused. "Charles and Sheila weren't that happy about her dating him, right?"

"Right. Sheila said he came from a bad background and he was trouble."

"I remember that part."

"And Meghan said that was why she was dating him."

"Because he was trouble?"

"That's what she told me once."

"What did she mean by that?"

"I don't know."

"Why do so many young people from good homes become fascinated with evil and hang around with the wrong crowd?"

"I think you're talking about our son Michael, not Meghan, John."

# Chapter 19
## *Wednesday, February 18*

In Winnipeg in mid-winter, the average daily high temperature is five degrees Fahrenheit, minus fifteen Celsius. The average daily low is minus ten Fahrenheit, minus twenty-five Celsius. The cold bottoms out in January, and by late February the temperatures have usually begun to rise, although for the most part still staying below the freezing mark. This year, an unseasonably strong and unseasonably late high pressure system had stalled over the Canadian prairies, pumping frigid cold air down from the Arctic and keeping nighttime temperatures hovering around minus thirty Celsius. The Manuels were still fighting the flu, and John Smyth was standing just inside the door of the classroom trying to catch his breath. He placed his hand over his mouth so the warmth would melt the ice that had formed in his mustache and beard. Most of the other students were already seated, dressed against the cold in sweaters and boots—except, of course, Pamela Wright, pulling on the hem of her tight black miniskirt so she wouldn't reveal too much as she sat down in the front row. A hand clapped Smyth on the shoulder.

"Come on, old man. The prof may not like you, but you can't stand here in the doorway all night."

Smyth started and then turned to see the big grin of Derek Uluchuk. "I'm not that old."

"Look around you. You're older than everyone else in the room, and you're even older than Professor Hemenhof."

"You can say the same thing about a kindergarten teacher—she's the oldest person in the room."

"It's all relative?"

"Yes, relative. I'm the same age as my wife, and she says she's young."

Derek laughed. "Good point."

"Besides, now that he knows me better, I think Professor Hemenhof is starting to respect me."

"Don't stand in the doorway, Mr. Smyth," Hemenhof commanded in a Humphrey Bogart voice. "Get in here and face the music."

The class laughed. Smyth and Derek moved quickly into the room and sat down in the front row near the door.

"Let's begin at the beginning," Hemenhof said. "Tonight we are going to look at structure in the mystery novel and then something about point of view. Some writers and critics insist that the murder must occur at the beginning of a mystery novel, preferably on the first page. This draws the reader in. It presents the puzzle which the reader can spend the rest of the book trying to solve. But in practice, particularly in a British cozy, the writer often spends up to half the book establishing the setting and the characters, the suspects, before committing the murder…to print." Hemenhof smiled. "In any case, there usually has to be something on the first page, a secondary mystery, or an interesting character, that will draw the reader in. Otherwise, the reader will stop reading before reaching the murder."

Hemenhof was pacing back and forth across the front of the room, making eye contact with each of the students in turn, like a skilled sheepdog making sure that all of the sheep remained with the flock and none was lost. "The opening ties in with point of view," he continued. "Many mysteries are told from the point of view of the omniscient narrator, with scenes changing all the time. Some follow the sleuth throughout the book seeing only what he or she sees and from his or her point of view. Most of these are still narrated in the third person, but Ross Macdonald has his lead character, Lew Archer, narrate the whole book. That is very hard to do, but it gives a sense of immediacy and focus to his books, even urgency. Ruth Rendell, on the other hand, often tells her stories mostly from the point of view of the killer, particularly her darker psychological stories she writes under the name Barbara Vine. There is no mystery about who did it, just the slow descent of the lead character into murder and death. She has obviously taken a university course in criminal psychology—or is perhaps psychotic herself." Hemenhof arched his eyebrows and paused. "Being a psychopath can be a quite enjoyable experience. You should all try it sometime."

The class snickered.

\*\*\*\*\*

Melting the snow from his mustache again, Smyth looked around the steamy interior of The Mystery of Chocolate, anticipating the tropical fruit truffle sitting in from of him. The cafe was crowded, but not as crowded as the previous week.

Brendan Mann seemed to have become a regular now. He seemed lost without Don Hamilton, his better-looking fellow athlete. He was sitting on the far side of the table, with Derek Uluchuk on one side of him and David Horcoff and Tyler Tapinski on the other. Betty Borden and Molly Pembroke were sitting on Smyth's right, on the other side of the empty chair left for Ruby.

"Roger was not related to anybody else in the group," Betty said. She seemed to have become the leader of the discussion of the clues. "Anybody have any ideas about what that clue means?"

"There are eight characters so far," Smyth suggested

"Right," Betty answered, "Rob, Roger, Larry, and Harry. Laura, Bev, Mary, and Alice. Four men and four women."

"But are those all of the characters?" Tyler asked.

"Good question," Betty answered.

"Picking up on tonight's lecture, this is obviously not one of those mysteries where the murder happens at the beginning," Smyth suggested. "We're halfway through the course, so that probably means Dr. Hemenhof has introduced the characters and the murder will happen soon, maybe next week, and then there will be more clues."

"That makes sense," Betty affirmed.

At that point, Ruby came in, gave John a peck on the cheek, and sat in the empty chair. John was the only one who stood up to greet her.

"Hi, everyone," she said brightly. "Have I missed much?"

"We were just discussing the clues," Betty answered. "Tonight's clue was 'Roger was not related to anybody else in the group,' so you didn't miss much there."

"I don't know," Derek quipped. "From the looks of things, I would say that Mrs. Smyth missed most of the old man's truffle."

"I saved half," Smyth said defensively."

"You know, you're right," Derek added. "Your wife is young."

"Thank you, I think," Ruby said.

78

"Can we get back to the clues?" Betty said irritably. "I think it might be helpful to try to figure out the various relationships. Clue number three mentions Larry's brother. Who is Larry's brother?"

They all consulted their notes. Ruby took a bite of John's truffle.

"It can't be Roger," Molly said, "because he is not related to anyone else."

"It's probably Harry," Derek suggested. "Larry and Harry, they're probably twins."

"It couldn't be Rob because Laura is Rob's sister and she dated both Larry and Harry. If Larry was Rob's brother, he would also be Laura's brother. That means she dated her brother."

"Eew!" Molly shivered.

"Why not?" Brendan spoke for the first time. "It's a mystery. Maybe there is something different going on."

"Absolutely," Tyler said. "We need to think outside the box. Why can't someone date his sister? You need to get past your small town morality."

There was an awkward silence.

Ruby broke the silence. "Molly, I thought someone said last week that you grew up on a farm."

Molly swallowed a piece of triple fudge layer cake. "My parents have a farm out near Boissevain."

"Oh, did you go to Boissevain Grace Evangelical Church? They would have received *Grace* magazine that John edits."

"Yes, we went to the church, and I think my parents got the magazine, but I'm afraid I've never read it."

"You're from Boissevain," Ruby continued, "and I know David is from Winnipeg. Where are the rest of you from?"

David looked shocked at being included in the conversation, but Tyler announced unexpectedly that he also was from Winnipeg, and the moment passed.

# Chapter 20

## Wednesday, February 25

"Are you sure you're not supposed to go to the university tonight?" Ruby was suspicious.

"Yes," John insisted. "Do you think I'm one of the kids making up excuses not to go to school?"

"Maybe," Ruby answered. "You don't like your teacher, and you complain about the class all the time."

"There is no class tonight," John said. "It's spring break."

"Spring break? It's minus twenty-five outside. It's not anywhere near spring."

"I know. It's called spring break because it's a break halfway through the spring semester."

"Spring semester? It's minus twenty-five outside."

"I've already been through this argument with the admissions counselor. It's called the spring semester because it's the semester that ends in the spring."

"That's silly."

"No, that's the university," John said. "The other name for it is ski week."

"That makes much more sense for a university in Winnipeg," Ruby answered.

"That's the unofficial name," John said. "Spring break is supposed to be a time when students who live far away can go home to their families for a visit and a time when students can do some extra work and get caught up on their reading and their assignments. But some students just use it to go on skiing trips."

"So what are you going to use your week for?" Ruby asked. "You don't ski."

"I should probably be working on the major essay for the class, but I haven't figured out a good topic to write on. Every topic I think of I don't think Professor Hemenhof would approve of."

Ruby smiled. "Why don't we just read our book tonight? You always say God often gives you the answer when you're busy doing something else."

# Chapter 21

*Friday, February 27*

"Thank you for agreeing to see us," Devorkian said.

"It was no trouble. I had a break in my schedule this morning," Charles Hall replied cautiously. "What did you want to talk to us about?" He was a tall, gray-haired man in a three-piece suit.

"There is no big agenda," Devorkian answered. "We are just going over the files for the young women who were murdered at the university and are re-interviewing all the witnesses."

"You haven't given up on finding who killed Meghan?" Sheila asked eagerly from her position on the sofa next to her husband.

"No, Mrs. Hall, we haven't given up," Devorkian answered.

"Does this mean you are making some progress toward finding the man responsible?" Charles asked stiffly.

Devorkian took a deep breath. "I am sorry. We haven't made any major breakthroughs," he said, "but that is how it often is with investigations. We keep working at it, going over the evidence, and eventually the pieces fall into place."

Charles looked thoughtful. "You think he is going to kill again this spring, don't you?"

Devorkian returned the look. "That is a possibility, but we would be doing this anyway. We still want to find who killed Meghan." He paused. "Now, can you tell me again what happened the night Meghan disappeared?"

It was Sheila who answered. "After supper, Meghan said she was going to the university to study. She had an exam the next day."

"Did she often do that?"

"Well, sometimes," Sheila answered. "She could study in her room, but sometimes she said there were too many distractions here and she would be more focused there."

"What time did she leave?"

"Just before seven. It only takes about ten minutes to get there." The Halls owned an expensive house in the affluent area just west of the university, not among the very expensive houses along the Assiniboine River, but near there, in an area where many professors lived.

"Did she say when she was going to return?"

"I told her to make sure she got in early so she could get some sleep because the exam was in the morning."

"And did she say she would do that?"

"She said she would be in by midnight."

"Did you consider that early?"

"No. She said she was going to study till about ten and then meet that boy at The Mystery of Chocolate."

"David Horcoff?"

"Yes. I told her not to meet him and to come home as soon as she finished studying."

"Did she agree to do that?"

"No."

"She didn't?"

"She was twenty-one, and she...well, even when she was younger, she wouldn't always obey me."

Devorkian turned suddenly to Charles. "What about you, Mr. Hall?"

"I wasn't home."

"Not even for supper?"

"No. I was working late, and I grabbed something to eat downtown."

"Did you often do that?"

"Sometimes."

Devorkian paused. "Why didn't you want your daughter to see David Horcoff?"

Sheila answered. "He wasn't a very nice boy. He had problems. He didn't come from a good family."

"He was trouble," Charles said bluntly. "He had already had some trouble with the law, and he would no doubt have more."

"Why did Meghan want to go out with him?"

"Who knows what gets into the mind of young girls?" Charles said hotly. "Why do they want to get involved with punks like David Horcoff? I don't know!"

"Did you know Meghan was going out with Horcoff that night, Mr. Hall?"

"Yes. Sheila told me."

"When?"

"After I got home."

Sheila made a small sobbing noise.

Devorkian pounced. "You don't agree, Mrs. Hall?"

She hesitated, then said, "I phoned him at work."

"When?"

"About seven-thirty."

"Did you talk to him?"

"No, I left a message."

"I didn't get it till the next day. I didn't know about it till I got home," Charles inserted.

"What time was that?"

"About ten-fifteen."

"About the time Meghan should have gotten home if she didn't go to meet David Horcoff?"

"Yes," Sheila said in a small voice.

"What did you do?"

"We were tired," Charles answered. "We went to bed."

"Weren't you worried about your daughter?"

"Meghan had been out with David Horcoff before, and she had never stayed out really late," Sheila said. "She was a good girl."

"How many times had she been out with David Horcoff?"

Sheila sighed. "I don't know. Three or four that I know of."

"That you know of," Devorkian repeated.

"Yes. She was at school all day, and she had friends. We didn't always know where she was. She was twenty-one. We trusted her."

"I'm not blaming you, Mrs. Hall," Devorkian said softly. "I'm just trying to understand. Did Meghan ever say why she was attracted to Horcoff?"

"No," Sheila answered. "She didn't want to talk about it, and that worried me a little. I think maybe she just felt sorry for him."

"Were you worried about Meghan that night?"

"Not greatly," Sheila answered. "She had always come in before."

"Did she have a cell phone? Could you have called her?"

Sheila looked at her husband. "Meghan had a cell phone," she said, "but it had stopped working that week, and she had been too busy with exams to get it replaced."

"When did you realize she hadn't come home?"

"The next morning."

"You didn't call the police?"

"We didn't think it was a police matter, Detective," Charles said. "She might have been studying with one of her other friends and decided to stay overnight. Girl friends, I mean. And if she was with Horcoff, well, we would have been very upset, but it was not a criminal matter. They were both over age."

"And we weren't absolutely sure she hadn't come home and then gone out again early to study before the exam," Sheila put in. "And then the police came..."

"That was just after noon?"

"Yes," Sheila answered. "When they came to the door, I thought it was Meghan coming home after her exam..."

*****

"What do you think we accomplished there?" Hosschuk asked, after having remained silent during the interrogation of the Halls.

"Other than upsetting the Halls, you mean?"

"Yeah."

Devorkian reflected as he turned the ignition and began driving away. "We confirmed that Charles Hall doesn't have an alibi for the time his daughter was murdered, and neither does his wife."

"Do you really suspect either of them? Did you get the feeling they were hiding something?"

Devorkian turned his head. "You're learning to see as well as listen. Yes, I got the impression they weren't telling us something, but whether it's relevant to the case, I don't know. Maybe Charles did get that phone message, went down to the university, had an argument with his daughter, and killed her. Maybe Charles lost his temper and broke the cell phone. I think we found a broken cell phone when we searched Meghan's room, by the way—it's in the files. Maybe Charles and Sheila aren't getting along and that's why he wasn't home that night. Maybe they are getting along too well and they were so busy making whoopie that night that they didn't even notice their daughter didn't come home. They might feel guilty about that."

"So do you suspect them or not?"

"It is important to keep an open mind. I'm not ruling them out as suspects. I don't think Charles could be guilty of the other murders, but I did say Meghan was different. She might have been murdered by a different killer."

"He was a lawyer. He might have gotten some inside information on the details of the first murders so he could copy the details."

"Good point." Devorkian drove in silence for a few moments. "No. I don't really think he did it. If David Horcoff was dead, I would arrest Charles Hall. But I can't see him killing his daughter, not that way."

"So, David Horcoff's still the main suspect?"

"For Meghan's murder, maybe."

"Not the others? He's got a record. Maybe he got to know all the victims and he was cultivating Meghan as his next one. Maybe it wasn't that Meghan was attracted to him but that he was attracted to Meghan."

Devorkian thought that over. "Maybe."

Hosschuk was silent for a few moments. "Anyway, it's good to have you back. I can't remember the last time you were off work that long."

"Two weeks in bed with the flu," Devorkian agreed. "Not the best holiday I've ever had. And considering the lack of progress we made today, I might as well have stayed home another week."

# Chapter 22

*Wednesday, March 4*

It was not yet spring, but the prolonged winter cold snap had finally broken. The daily high temperature had climbed to near the freezing point, the sun was shining, and Winnipeggers, acclimatized to winter, were now walking about with one or two buttons on their parkas unbuttoned, basking in the unaccustomed warmth of temperatures that would have had Floridians running for cover. The snow had not begun to melt yet, but it had compacted, and a few bare patches of sidewalk were starting to appear. Now that the weather was better, the Manuels were too, and John Smyth was back to driving to class once again. He was sitting in the front row once again, next to Derek and five seats from Pamela Wright.

"Is it just a coincidence that you all decided to take this class?" Professor Hemenhof was saying. He paused. "Coincidence. It is the lifeblood of mystery novels. Agatha Christie's Miss Marple is an old lady who lives in the tiny hamlet of St. Mary Mead, but it just so happens that a number of murders take place in this village, and Miss Marple solves all of them. Think about that. A quiet village in the countryside with a murder rate higher than any inner city in the US. And this doesn't just happen in St. Mary Mead. Everywhere this woman travels, people drop dead all around her. After a while, you can imagine people screaming in terror, 'Run for cover! Hide the children! Miss Marple is coming to town!'"

The students laughed.

"If the hero of a mystery series is a detective or a policeman, it makes sense that he or she would constantly be involved with murder. The cases would naturally come to the detective or the policeman as part of his or her job. But many mystery writers choose to have amateur heroes. And if the hero is an amateur such as Miss Marple, it would be a remarkable coincidence for her to even be involved with more than one murder, let alone solve more than one. For instance, has anyone here ever been involved with a murder, as an acquaintance of the murderer or the victim, as a witness—or perhaps as a murderer?"

The class tittered nervously.

Looking at Betty, Hemenhof added, "Having the same name as a murderer doesn't count. If you have had actual contact with a murder, raise your hand."

Three people, Rachel Chu, David Horcoff, and John Smyth, raised their hands.

"Now, have any of you ever been involved with a second murder that occurred at a different time or place? See, that just doesn't happen in real life—" He stopped, glaring at John Smyth in the front row, with his hand tentatively raised halfway. There was a long pause. "Mr. Smyth. I might have known. I pegged you for a serial killer from the start."

There was nervous laughter.

Hemenhof returned to the lectern, glanced at his notes, and continued. "Coincidence is a common feature in mystery novels, not just in having the same character solve crimes, but also in the clues and other relationships. For instance, the hero happens to overhear a conversation which provides a vital clue. Or he happens to read a newspaper article about forged paintings just before investigating a murder at an art gallery. Or she makes a wrong turn in the old mansion and comes across the mate to the glove that was dropped at the murder scene. Or it turns out that while the butler was murdering the lord in the library, the parlor maid was admitting that she had been a suspect in the murder of a previous employer, and the cook is the long-lost daughter of the lord's first wife. How can we explain such coincidences?

"For one thing, we can just accept such coincidences as necessary to make intricate plots work—and, of course, mystery plots are by their nature more intricate than other plots. This is called the willing suspension of disbelief. That is, you know that what you are reading is fiction, it didn't happen, it probably couldn't happen even, but you ignore these rational objections so that you can enjoy the book. That is not a very satisfactory answer, but sometimes it is all we are left with.

"Another argument is that coincidences happen all the time. You know the theory that there are only six steps of separation for any two people in the world? You are a friend of a man who wrote a book about a Russian named Temptkin, who has a third cousin from the village of Plushkovo, whose mayor is a friend of another man named Petrovsky, who is a fourth cousin to your girlfriend's aunt. Such coincidences happen. That is why we have the expression, 'Small world.' There are billions and billions of interactions in the world, and sooner or later one of these will make a bizarre connection. Golfers tee off millions of times each year in North America, but the tee shot that makes the news is the hole in one. You throw many darts at the dart board, but the one that you remember is the bull's-eye. In any murder, there are many clues and many people interacting with the clues, but the only interaction that gets noticed is the one that makes a connection. There are thousands of details in the detective's life every day, but the only ones worth reporting are the ones that solve the crime. The police officer interrogates hundreds of witnesses, so it is no surprise that one of them actually saw something significant. And there are many cases where no one makes the connection and the murder is therefore not solved—but no one writes books about those cases."

Many of the students were nodding in agreement. John Smyth raised his hand.

Hemenhof sighed. "Yes, Mr. Smyth."

Smyth took a deep breath and then began. "Chuck Colson says that good stories affirm that some force is at work rewarding good and punishing evil. Couldn't it be that all of life is connected and has a purpose? So the connections we see are just the connections that are already there. And murder mysteries and other good stories just reflect that reality."

Hemenhof smiled. "You've been reading Clive Staple."

"Who's Clive Staple?"

"Don't be difficult, Mr. Smyth. Clive Staple is a literature professor at some two-bit Bible college down in the States. He wrote a book called *Murder, Mysteries and Morality,* as I'm sure you know, Mr. Smyth. Among other things, he argues just what you said, that mysteries reflect the order and purpose that already exists in the universe. But it's nonsense, Mr. Smyth. Clive Staple is wrong. Mystery novels thrive on coincidences, and they have well-developed plots leading to conclusive answers. But they are fiction, Mr. Smyth. Organized coincidence is a literary device, not reality. Life is not like that. In spite of some instances of causality, human life has no overriding purpose. Human life is a series of random occurrences with no discernible pattern or purpose."

"I-I've never heard of Clive Staple," Smyth stammered. "If we came to the same conclusion, maybe it's because we both saw a pattern that really exists." He paused. "Or maybe it's just a coincidence."

The students laughed.

Hemenhof looked disconcerted, but after a moment he smiled. "Was that a joke, Mr. Smyth? Maybe there's hope for you yet. Even if you're wrong."

*****

"I told you I thought Professor Hemenhof was starting to like me," Smyth said.

Derek Uluchuk looked incredulous. "You think?"

"Well, respect me at least."

The group around the table was silent. At last, Derek spoke. "Give up, old man. I don't think so."

Tyler Tapinski said forcefully, "You just don't get it. It's not a question of liking. Professor Hemenhof is a scientific, objective, rational thinker. It doesn't matter whether he likes Mr. Smyth but whether Mr. Smyth does good work in this class and understands the course. Professor Hemenhof will mark him fairly. He'll mark all of us fairly."

Betty Borden quickly changed the subject. "What do you think of this week's clue—'Rob and Laura had a fight. Rob stormed off, leaving Laura alone. An hour later, the killer struck.'?"

There was more silence.

Derek spoke up again. "Well, the old man was right. He said last week the murder would happen soon."

"But we don't even know who was murdered," Molly Pembroke complained.

"Sure we do," Derek said. "It was Laura."

"Or Rob," Betty countered.

"Or maybe one of them did it?" Tyler said.

"Maybe they had nothing to do with it." It was the first time David Horcoff had contributed to the discussion in the group, and his words were greeted by a shocked silence.

90

"I think David is right," Derek said. "We don't really know much more than we did before."

There was another pause. The conversation seemed stuck this night, as awkward and hesitant as a first date.

Derek suddenly asked John, "Is Mrs. Smyth coming tonight? You didn't get another chair."

"No, she only came the last two weeks to pick me up. I normally drive, but she needed the car the last couple of weeks."

Derek swore vehemently and then to the shocked faces around the table added, "What? I figure she is the only one of us who had a chance of figuring it out."

"Speaking of absentees," Betty said, looking at Brendan Mann, "why doesn't your friend Don Hamilton come to our group?"

Brendan shrugged. "He, uh, had a date."

"He seems to have a date every Wednesday," Betty suggested.

"Probably with that ho, Pamela Wright," Molly said. "She never comes either."

Brendan Mann scowled.

# Chapter 23
## Friday, March 6

He was sitting behind the large oak desk. Both sides of the room were lined floor to ceiling with neat bookcases, and the back wall contained a large window which looked out over parking lot D and the endowment lands beyond it. With his broad shoulders, steel gray hair, conservative tie, and expensive sports coat, Don Henderson was a distinguished-looking man.

"Thank you for agreeing to see us, Dr. Henderson," Devorkian said. He and Hosschuk were seated in the uncomfortable chairs across from the professor.

"It's no problem. How can I help you?"

Devorkian deliberately took his time answering. "Dr. Henderson, two years ago, when Lorraine Malthus was murdered, you approached the Winnipeg Police Department with the suggestion that the murder might have something to do with the Malthusian theory."

"So that's what this is about. Are you still working on that case?"

"The case is not yet solved. Therefore, we're still working on it," Devorkian said evenly. "Why did you do that?"

"Go to the police? Oh, I just thought it might help. I assumed that it would be helpful if the police had as much information as possible. I teach English literature, poetry mostly, and so I deal with symbols and hidden meanings. When I read that a student named Malthus had been murdered, I wondered if her death might be related to Malthus's theory, if it might have been intended to be symbolic. After all, since she was a student and the murder happened near campus, it was possible that the murderer was connected to the university and therefore might think in terms of symbols."

"So you think the murderer was someone from the university? Why?"

"There was no particular reason. It was just that she was a student and she was killed near the campus. I don't have any particular knowledge."

"Are you sure? You don't have a guess about who murdered Lorraine Malthus? There's not someone you're suspicious about?"

"No."

"Do you know anyone who is interested in Malthus's theory?"

Henderson was silent a moment. "The theory has been discussed and studied here, but I can't think of anyone who had a particular interest."

"Where was it discussed?"

"Oh, I don't remember. It comes up in class occasionally, and sometimes in discussions among faculty. There was no one who studied it specifically that I know of or who talked about it frequently."

"Do you still think the murder might have something to do with Malthus's theory?"

Henderson paused. "I don't know. That's for you to decide. I just raised it as a possibility. It doesn't seem as likely to me now as it did then. I thought about it for a while before coming to the police. I wasn't sure it was important, but I thought I should suggest it anyway and let you decide if it meant anything. If there was something in it, I didn't want to be responsible for not saying anything."

"Did you know Lorraine Malthus?" Devorkian asked suddenly.

"No."

"You didn't teach her?"

"I don't think so."

"You're not sure?"

"Detective, I have taught hundreds of students every year for the past twenty-five years. I don't remember them all."

"Her picture was in the paper, and you obviously read the paper. You should have remembered."

"I'm sorry. I don't."

"What about Astrid Andersson?"

"Who?"

"The second student who was murdered, a year later."

"Oh, yes. No, I didn't know her."

"Are you sure?"

"Not entirely. As I said, I have taught thousands of students."

"She was a first-year student. You would have taught her the year she died."

"Probably not, then."

"Meghan Hall?" Devorkian asked casually.

"Did I know her? Yes. She attended the same church I do. I know her parents, and I talked to her a few times there. She also took two of my courses."

"So you remember her?"

"Yes."

"But not the others?"

"Detective, why are you asking questions that I have already answered? Do you suspect me of being involved in the murders?"

"I'll ask the questions," Devorkian said smoothly. "You have a good view of the endowment lands from this office. You could see who goes in and out from here."

"I suppose, if I didn't have anything to do but stare out the window all day," Henderson said coldly.

Devorkian ignored his tone. "You've been teaching here twenty-five years?"

"Yes, about that."

"You seem in pretty good shape."

"I work out at the gym three days a week. Teaching is a sedentary profession. One has to be disciplined and exercise regularly in order to remain healthy."

"Do you ever walk in the endowment lands?"

"Not often."

"But sometimes?"

"Maybe a few times a year. In the summer, if I need something from the store, occasionally I will walk through to the mall on the other side."

"But not for pleasure."

"No."

"You didn't happen to go in the night Lorraine Malthus was murdered?"

"Certainly not. I don't go wandering around the woods at night. I'm not foolish."

"Did you see anyone go in that night?"

"From my office? It's not likely. I'm not usually here in the evenings, except when I teach an evening class. If I have work to do in the evenings, I usually do it in my office at home."

"Were you here the night Lorraine Malthus was murdered?"

"That was two years ago! I have no idea what I was doing that night. Most likely I was at home."

"Where do you live?"

"Surely, Detective, you know that already. I live on Western Boulevard."

"That's only a few blocks west of the university."

"About a mile actually. A lot of professors live in that area."

"No one else can afford to," Hosschuk said scornfully, speaking for the first time.

Devorkian smiled. "How about the night Astrid Andersson died?"

"I have no idea. Probably at home."

"Any witnesses?"

"Probably not."

"And the night Meghan Hall was murdered?"

Henderson was silent.

"Dr. Henderson?"

"That night I remember. I was here till about eleven o'clock. Some of my students had written an exam that day, and I was marking papers."

"I thought you said you never worked here at night."

"I said I rarely worked here at night. That night was an exception. I-I just didn't feel like going home."

"Did anyone see you here?"

Again Henderson hesitated. "No, I don't think so. I kept my door closed most of the way. I saw some people pass by the door, but I didn't talk to anyone."

"What time did you see them?"

"I don't know. Various times. Mostly earlier in the evening, around nine or so. I think the janitor was around after that. I really wasn't paying attention."

"Did you see anyone in particular, anyone you recognized?"

Henderson stared at Devorkian for a few moments as if he was thinking.

"How do you remember where you were that night?" Devorkian asked suddenly.

"Because I knew Meghan, and I was here. When I heard about it the next day, I kept wondering whether, if I had turned around and looked out the window, I might have seen something and might have been able to prevent her murder."

"Are you married, professor?"

Henderson froze. "I assume you already know the answer to that question too. I was married twenty-seven years, but my wife died."

"Three years ago in April."

"Yes."

"Don't you find that an odd coincidence?"

"What?"

"The first student was killed almost a year after your wife died."

Henderson was silent.

"And two years after her death, two students died."

"Are you suggesting I had something to do with the murders?"

"Did you?"

"No."

"Do you miss your wife?"

Henderson's throat caught. "Yes. Adrienne was a wonderful woman. I loved her. I miss her terribly."

"So you're lonely."

Henderson made a futile gesture but said nothing.

"Do you ever date students?"

"What?"

"Students. You're a good-looking man, fit. Students would look up to you. Did you ever date one?"

"No. That would be unethical."

"What do people call you for short?"

The question had been unexpected. "Uh, my friends usually call me Don."

"Anyone ever call you DH?"

"DH?"

"Those are your initials, aren't they?"

"Yes, but no one ever calls me that."

"Do you know anyone who is called DH?"

Henderson thought a moment. "No, I can't think of anyone."

Devorkian was silent for a full minute. "Is there anything else you'd like to tell us?"

Henderson also paused. "No, there isn't," he said firmly.

Devorkian was silent for another full minute. "If you think of anything, call me." He placed his card on Henderson's desk. "Thank you, Dr. Henderson," he said, rising.

*****

Their car was on the edge of parking lot D, facing into the endowment lands. They were walking toward it.

Hosschuk said, "You pushed him pretty hard."

"Yes, I did."

"He stood up to it pretty well."

"Yes, he did."

"So what do you think?"

"I don't think he's telling us everything he knows," Devorkian smiled. "But whether he killed those women I don't know. He could have. He's older but a good-looking man. Young women away from home for the first time might be attracted to him. He was married a long time and would have been lonely for some female companionship."

"You're convinced he loved his wife?"

"Oh, yes, unless he's a tremendous actor. Those were genuine tears."

"And she died of cancer, so he couldn't have killed *her*."

"No, but grief may have pushed him over the edge."

"He's certainly strong enough to have strangled the victims."

"He is that."

"What do you think of his theory that if he had looked out of his window, he might have seen Meghan Hall and prevented her death?"

Devorkian shrugged. "Probably wishful thinking. But I wish somebody had looked out a window and seen something."

"But who? There's probably nobody around this place after midnight."

Devorkian paused. "Maybe there's someone we're not thinking of."

# Chapter 24

## Wednesday, March 11

John Smyth's old gray station wagon pulled into parking lot D and ground to a halt in one of the last remaining parking spaces. A black Lexus pulled in right after him and parked two stalls down. Professor Hemenhof got out of the driver's side, and another man got out of the other. He was wearing a black leather dress coat and was about the same height but with dark, bushy hair and a black goatee. He walked with an easy grace, like an elf. Smyth, fumbling to lock the anti-theft device on the steering wheel and collect his books, clambered out of the station wagon and followed the two men into the Riel Building. He felt like a child following his teacher to class or a puppy following his master.

Once inside, the two men turned to the left and went up a set of stairs toward the second floor, while Smyth headed down the hall toward lecture hall 131. He paused to maneuver around a green-uniformed janitor who was making long, sweeping passes along the hallway floor with a wide industrial vacuum. Derek Uluchuk fell into step beside him.

"Hello, old man," Derek said. "Back again, eh?"

Smyth smiled. "Good evening, Derek. Did you see that man with Professor Hemenhof?"

"Yeah."

"Do you know who he is?"

"Why do you want to know?"

"Just curiosity. I'm a writer, remember? He looked interesting."

"That was Professor Kingston."

"Professor Kingston..." The name sounded familiar.

"He teaches Greek and Latin literature."

"Oh, yes, he's the..." Smyth stopped.

"The gay guy? Sure."

They were early, and the other students were straggling in after them. The students still sat in pretty much the same positions as they had the first week, except that Smyth now sat next to Derek, and Molly and Betty were sitting together. Brendan Mann and Don Hamilton were still sitting together in the middle right, Tyler Tapinski and Pamela Wright were still sitting separately in the front row, and David Horcoff was still sitting alone in the back row.

Professor Hemenhof came in, set down his books and notes, and began pacing back and forth, looking at the expectant students. "My, you do enjoy murder, don't you?"

As was often the case, the students weren't quite sure where the professor was going.

"That is a quote," he said. "Anybody recognize it?"

There were no takers. "A quote," he continued, "from E.X. Giroux, aka Doris Shannon, a Canadian who wrote mysteries set in England. The quote is from her last book, *A Death for a Dodo*, and it is a question asked of her sleuth, Robert Forsythe. He responds coldly, 'I loathe murder, but I like puzzles. I also believe in justice and strongly feel that any person who takes a life must pay.' It was perhaps Shannon's justification for spending her life writing mysteries, a defense of her interest in murder."

Hemenhof stopped his words and his pacing. He was a master of the dramatic pause. "Clive Staple," he continued, "in 1995 wrote a book called *Murder, Mysteries and Morality*, considered by some people to be a classic. He argues that people write and read mystery stories for two main reasons. One is that mysteries reinforce moral values—they affirm that there is such a thing as right and wrong, that those who do wrong will be caught and punished, and that justice will prevail in the end. The other reason for reading mysteries, Staple says, is that they affirm that there is such a thing as truth and that we can definitely find the truth. He points out that people read mysteries not just to see justice done but to know 'whodunit'."

Hemenhof paused again. "Clive Staple is a professor at some deservedly obscure Bible college in the southern United States. Doris Shannon was almost seventy when she wrote her last book—and her views are decidedly old-fashioned. And they are wrong. Increasingly in modern mysteries, the solution to the crime remains ambiguous. And even if the sleuth himself uncovers whodunit, he may choose to keep that knowledge secret from the authorities since the murder was justified. In some cases, the sleuth may even commit murder himself. Modern mysteries reveal that truth and justice are far more ambiguous than previous generations assumed, and people read those books anyway. Modern psychology has taught us that arguments such as the pursuit of truth and morality are rationalizations for our real motives, which are primarily selfish. As writers such as Stephen King have proven, people really read mysteries, suspense stories, and horror stories because they are fascinated with evil and blood, with violence and with experiencing things that they wouldn't normally get to experience in their everyday lives.

"For religious fanatics like Clive Staple and Mr. Smyth here, old-fashioned mysteries may offer the comforting illusion that justice will prevail. But it *is* an illusion. The fact is that there is no such thing as justice. Most criminals are never caught, and the ones that are caught are not given a just penalty for their crimes—and who can define what a just penalty would be anyway?"

In the silence, Smyth raised his hand. "Do you really believe that?" he asked.

Hemenhof turned his full attention on Smyth. "This is university, not Bible college, Mr. Smyth. It doesn't matter what I believe. I'm trying to get you to think."

"In that case, I *think* mysteries affirm the truth that justice will prevail in the end, if not in this world, then in the next."

"Ah, the last refuge of the religious. When they are given irrefutable proof that they are wrong, they simply assert that the evidence will be reversed in the next life, an assertion that can never be tested scientifically. When thinking leads to a conclusion they don't like, they choose to believe the opposite."

Smyth sat silently, feeling intimidated by the forcefulness of the professor's reply, unable to decide what to say next.

*****

The weather had warmed to the point that Winnipeggers no longer walked with their heads buried in parka hoods and scarves, even in the evening. Because of the narrowness of the sidewalks, they broke into pairs. Smyth found himself walking beside Derek Uluchuk. Tyler

Tapinski and Brendan Mann were taking the lead, followed by Molly Pembroke and Betty Borden, while David Horcoff walked alone at the rear. It seemed to be his natural position in life. Smyth was thinking about that and how he had made a connection to Meghan Hall.

"Do you?"

Smyth suddenly realized that Derek had been talking and had asked him a question. "I'm very sorry, Derek. My mind wandered for a moment."

Derek scowled. "It's alright. It's to be expected in the elderly."

Smyth laughed. "I'm not that old."

Derek's face showed deep concern. "It's the hearing then, is it?"

They both laughed then.

Derek continued. "I was saying that you don't still think Professor Hemenhof is starting to like you, do you?"

"It's not a matter of him liking me. It's a matter of discussing ideas and learning to understand."

"You're quoting Tyler."

"Yes."

"Well, I don't like her!"

Smyth and Derek were shocked into silence. It was a snippet of conversation, spoken forcefully by Molly Pembroke in front of them.

"But you want to be like her," Betty responded.

"No, I don't! She's so phony, with those short skirts, all that make-up, and those silly wigs. She probably has other false parts too."

"But men like that sort of thing. We don't want to be like Pamela Wright, but we want men like Don Hamilton to like us. But they won't unless we become what we don't like."

"I detect a hint of jealousy, I think," Derek whispered to Smyth.

Smyth was thinking. Tall, big-boned, brown-haired Molly and sharp-faced Betty were right. Most men would not look at them twice, and yet they were reasonably good students with pleasant enough personalities. They surely envied women like Pamela Wright, but was Pamela any happier than they were? Would they really want to trade places with her?

They had arrived at The Mystery of Chocolate. When they had collected their overpriced and overly caloried desserts and drinks, they found a table in the crowded restaurant.

"Let's talk about tonight's clue," Betty said in a business-like tone. She consulted a piece of paper. "It's 'Larry wondered if his brother had done it because he was jealous.' Anybody have any ideas about that?"

"I think this clue confirms what we were talking about before," Tyler said, looking at his own notes. "There are four men and four women. We decided before that Larry's brother can't be Roger because Roger's not related to anyone, and it's probably not Rob because Rob is dating Laura, and Laura is Larry's brother. That means that Harry must be Larry's brother. This new clue tells us that Harry, Larry's brother, did it, and it gives us a motive, jealousy. This assignment isn't that hard if you think about it logically. I think we're going to solve it by the time we have all the clues."

"But we don't know for sure Harry is the brother," Betty answered. "And the clue doesn't say that the brother did it, only that Larry thinks he did it."

"Did what?" Brendan asked. "It doesn't say that the brother killed anyone, only that he did something. When we talk about 'doing it,' we mean sex. Maybe this is a what you call a…"

"A red herring?" Betty asked.

"Yeah," Brendan continued. "Maybe the brother didn't have anything to do with the murder. He was just having sex with someone or doing something else."

"But this is a murder puzzle," Molly contributed, "and we only get thirteen clues. It has to mean the murder."

"Probably," Betty agreed. "But who did he murder?"

"And who was he jealous of?" Molly asked.

"This clue proves one thing anyway," Derek said. "If Larry suspects someone else, that means that Larry didn't do it. We can at least eliminate him as a suspect."

There were murmurs of agreement and head nodding.

"Hey. I would say this assignment has got us doing what Professor Hemenhof wants us to be doing," Tyler said. "We're thinking logically."

There was an embarrassed silence. No one looked at John Smyth.

"If nobody has anything else to say about the assignment, I would like to solve another mystery," Molly said. "Remember at the start of the term, we had that dorky assignment about why we were taking the course?"

The others nodded. Smyth grimaced.

"So we know why some of us are taking the course," Molly continued. "Why are the rest of us taking it?"

"It looked like some easy credits," Brendan said.

"You're majoring in phys ed, right?" Molly asked.

"Yeah. So?"

"Nothing."

"I took the class because I'd heard Dr. Hemenhof was a good lecturer and it was an interesting course," Derek said.

"Me, too," Tyler said. "Professor Hemenhof is a good prof."

"Why did you take the course, Molly?" Betty asked.

Molly shrugged. "I like reading mysteries. I'd already read half the books for the course."

"You didn't put that on your assignment?" Betty asked.

"No, I talked about enjoying mental puzzles and wanting to sharpen my mind. I got a B." Molly paused. "David, why did you take the course?"

Immediately the atmosphere crackled with tension. Smyth wondered whether David would run out as he had before or whether he would explode with anger.

After several long moments, David said in a quiet but taut voice, "Last year, my friend Meghan Hall was murdered. I took the course because I want to understand why."

"I don't think this course will help you with that," Molly said sympathetically.

# Chapter 25

## Friday, March 13

The two-story house was fronted with dirty gray stucco accented with peeling dark brown trim. There were no shrubs in the front yard, and the house was situated in a dingy neighborhood surrounded by more dingy houses.

For several moments, the two men sat in their car and watched the house. Nothing was stirring. Finally, they got out and walked up to the front door. Doorbell wires hung from a small hole in the front door frame. The muscular blond-haired one pounded on the door with his fist. After a few moments, there was a click, and the dark brown door creaked halfway open. A pale-faced young man with unnaturally black hair and large earrings on both eyebrows peered around the edge of the door.

"We're here to see David Horcoff," the tall man in the elegant coat said.

The young man looked doubtfully at the two big men on the doorstep, then shrugged and opened the door. He was wearing a black tee-shirt and black jeans. He was standing in a dark front hall, with some stairs leading up to the right, and two closed dark brown doors to the left. The hall itself led back to a tiny kitchen.

The tall man sniffed. The place was permeated by a foul odor, or combination of foul odors. Like many other such places, the house had been broken up into tiny bedrooms, except for the upstairs bathroom and downstairs kitchen. There was no living room, and the impoverished young men and women who lived here would only meet if they bumped into one another while going out through the hall or while cooking their separate meals in the tiny kitchen. It was not a community, but a warren of burrows for the truly alone.

The pale young man in black jerked his head in the direction of the stairs. "Second door on the left." As the two men started up the stairs, he pushed the front door shut and slammed the deadbolt home.

The muscular blond-haired man knocked vigorously on the door of the room. It had apparently not quite been latched because it swung openly immediately. David Horcoff, sitting on the bed, looked startled, like a deer caught in headlights. Recovering quickly, he shoved the object in his hand into the black backpack sitting on his lap.

"David Horcoff?" the tall one asked.

Horcoff nodded.

"I am Detective Devorkian, and this is Sergeant Hosschuk. We'd like to ask you a few questions."

Horcoff remained sitting on the bed. There was no other surface in the room where the policemen could sit, so they remained standing. This gave them the advantage of allowing them to tower over the man on the bed.

"Tell us about Meghan Hall," Devorkian continued.

Horcoff shrugged. "She was nice. She was murdered." His voice was deep and gravelly, but with a trace of a whine.

"Did you kill her?"

Horcoff seemed to have been expecting this. "No."

"You were supposed to meet her the night she died."

"In The Mystery of Chocolate. I waited almost an hour. She never came."

"You were supposed to meet her at ten, right? What time did you get there?"

Horcoff shrugged. "Maybe quarter after."

"Why were you late?"

Horcoff froze and didn't say anything.

"Why were you late?"

"It just took me longer to get there than I expected. I was walking."

"Where were you walking from?"

Horcoff hesitated, a look of indecision on his face. "From here."

Devorkian thought a moment. "That would be what, four or five kilometers?"

Horcoff shrugged.

"What route did you take?"

"Across the bridge, across campus."

"Through the endowment lands?"

Horcoff shrugged. "So?"

"So maybe you met Meghan on the way in the endowment lands and killed her, and that's why you were late," Hosschuk put in.

"She drove," Horcoff answered.

"Her car was found in parking lot D next to the endowment lands," Devorkian said. "Maybe you met her there, pulled her into the woods, and killed her."

Horcoff didn't answer. There was a light burning in his eyes, but Devorkian wasn't sure if it was anger or fear or some other emotion. "If she had a car, why didn't she pick you up?" he asked.

"This is a bad neighborhood."

"What exactly was your relationship with Meghan?"

"We were friends."

"Boyfriend girlfriend?"

"We went out a few times."

"Where did you go?"

"Coffee mostly. A movie once."

"How long had you been dating?'

"A couple of months."

"How did you meet her?"

"In a class."

"What class?"

"A couple of classes, creative writing and history."

"What history?" Devorkian demanded sharply.

"European thought in the eighteenth and nineteenth centuries."

"When was that?"

"The fall term, before…"

"Did you talk to her then?"

"Not much."

"Then how'd you start going out a few months later?"

"In the cafeteria. She sat down next to me, she remembered me from class, and we started talking."

"So she was attracted to you first?"

Horcoff shrugged.

"Why was she attracted to you?"

"I don't know," Horcoff said sullenly. "She just was."

"What did you talk about when you were having coffee?"

"Classes. Movies. Books. Life."

"What were you planning to talk about the night she didn't show up? Was there anything special about that night?"

Horcoff shook his head.

"How did you meet Astrid Andersson?"

Horcoff hesitated. "Ambrosia Club."

"Where?"

"Ambrosia Club." Horcoff waved his hand. "A pub on campus."

"When did you start dating her?"

"I didn't. We just talked a couple of times in the pub."

Devorkian nodded. "Where did you meet Lorraine Malthus?"

"I never met her."

"But you know who she is."

"Everybody knows who she is."

"But not everybody went to the same high school as she did."

Horcoff shrugged. "I'd heard the name, but she was a couple of years ahead of me. It was a big school. I didn't know her."

"So you'd never met her before you killed her?" Hosschuk asked suddenly.

Horcoff looked startled, but recovered. "I didn't kill her either."

"How can you afford to go to university, David?"

"Icky."

"Icky?" Hosschuk repeated.

"An Inner-City Initiative grant?" Devorkian asked."

Horcoff nodded. "And I work."

"Where?"

"Cleaner at the university on weekends."

"A janitor?"

"Part-time."

"What are you studying?"

"English."

"Why?"

"I like it."

"What are you going to do with your degree?"

"Write." Horcoff shrugged. "Meghan thought…"

107

"Meghan thought what?"

"Nothing."

"Meghan thought what?" Devorkian repeated.

Horcoff set his jaw. "Meghan thought I should be a teacher," he said defiantly. "Meghan said I could be anything I want. But you think because I grew up in north Winnipeg all I can be is a murderer!"

*****

"We can connect him to two of the dead women," Hosschuk offered when they were back in their car. "That's something."

"Yes, but we cannot connect him to any of the murders," Devorkian answered.

"And we can't directly connect him to Lorraine Malthus."

"Except that they went to the same high school, and we know he studied the Malthusian theory."

"We do?"

"Yes, we do," Devorkian said. "He studied European thought in the eighteenth century, and that course would almost certainly have included some mention of Malthus and his theory."

"Okay."

"The only problem is that he studied Malthus the fall before Astrid and Meghan were killed, but the fall *after* Lorraine was killed."

Hosschuk was silent. "Maybe he took the course because he had already killed her."

"Maybe. In April, when Lorraine was killed, he would probably already have chosen his courses for the next year. Maybe he had already come across the theory and signed up for the course precisely for that reason. The question is: how do we prove it?"

More silence. "What do you think he slipped into his backpack when we walked in?"

"Drugs would be one guess, but it could also be a stolen wallet, a book, or just about anything else."

"If you suspected it might be something illegal, then why didn't you search his backpack?"

"We were there to ask him about the murders. We didn't have probable grounds for searching the backpack, and anything we found would be eliminated as evidence."

"Could we get a search warrant to search his room?"

"On what grounds? And what would we find? Do you really think he brought any of those women to that house?"

"Maybe he took a souvenir."

"The only thing missing that we know of is Lorraine Malthus's purse, and we think that was not taken as a souvenir but to take away evidence. My guess is that it is long gone by now."

"What about Meghan Hall's purity ring?"

Devorkian froze. "I had forgotten about that." He thought for a moment. "But what Horcoff put into his backpack looked bigger than that."

"Maybe he's got it in a box."

"Maybe. If anybody took Meghan Hall's purity ring, it's not surprising it would be Horcoff."

# Chapter 26
## Wednesday, March 18

It is easy to drive in Winnipeg in the winter. The prevailing west winds don't have much moisture left once they have blown all the way across the Canadian prairies to reach the city, and there is neither an abundance of rain in the summer nor an abundance of snow in the winter. But what snow falls, stays, as the temperature remains solidly below zero for two months or more. Because of this, the fallen snow does not melt and refreeze, turning to ice. It remains crystalline. Even with six inches or more of snow on the streets after a recent snowfall, perhaps mixed with sand laid down by work crews, it is still possible to drive, slowly but safely, much like driving on a beach.

Spring is another matter. As the temperature rises, the snow begins to melt during the day and refreeze into new, harder shapes at night. Throughout the winter, the city is well-equipped to remove snow from the streets with plows, front-end loaders and dump trucks, but it rarely touches the back alleys that run behind the houses on most blocks in the middle of the city. Here the snow remains, packed hard like beach sand by the passing traffic, a foot or two deep. When spring comes, the snow becomes soft, and the cars sink deeper and deeper during the day, creating deep ruts. The ruts freeze overnight, and when morning comes, cars backing out of garages across the alleys can become stranded, their front wheels in one rut, their back wheels in the other rut and their bodies sitting on the frozen snow between.

Thus begins the annual ritual. Homeowners who have ignored the snow in the alleyways all winter, now have to do something about it. That something is shoveling the slushy snow off to the side during the warm daytime hours and making sure the storm drains are chopped open to receive the melt water. It was a beautifully warm spring afternoon with the temperature a few degrees above zero. John Smyth, in knee-high rubber boots, was spending an hour hacking away at the stubborn ice and slush, sweating profusely in a light jacket. He stopped for a breather, wondering idly whether life might be easier somewhere else. But he rejoiced, too, in the fresh air, the healthy exercise, the warm sun, and the glorious return of life after a long, cold winter. He was feeling hopeful, as if things were going to take a turn for the better.

*****

Once the sun had gone down, however, the crisp clear air turned cold again, and the thawing life froze hard.

"Why do almost all mystery stories revolve around murder?" Professor Hemenhof asked. "There are exceptions, of course. Sherlock Holmes solved a few crimes involving stolen jewels and stolen military plans, but those involved organized crime, international conspiracies, and the potential loss of many lives. And in the past some mysteries for teens may also have avoided scary things like murder, but modern teen mysteries revel in murder, and the gorier the better. The fact remains that ninety-nine percent of all mysteries involve murder. Why is that? S.S. Van Dine, author of the Philo Vance mysteries, stated, 'There simply must be a corpse in a detective novel, and the deader the corpse the better. No lesser crime than murder will suffice. Three hundred pages is far too much pother for a crime other than murder.'"

Hemenhof raised his eyebrows ludicrously high as he finished, and the students laughed.

"Clive Staple," Hemenhof continued, "Mr. Smyth's fellow religious fanatic, goes even farther. Staple agrees that mysteries involve murder because they must be about something important. But he goes on to say, 'Ironically, murder mysteries, because they say murder is wrong, confirm the great value of human life made in the image of God.'"

The classroom was silent.

Hemenhof continued, "Van Dine is correct. Mysteries involve murder because they must be about something important. But Clive Staple, as usual, is wrong. We don't read mysteries because they affirm life, but because they take us across the forbidden frontier, to revel in death and blood while maintaining the illusion that we are doing it for perfectly respectable reasons. We read mysteries for the same reasons some people join the military or the police force—so they can kill with impunity, so they can revel in the commission of murder."

*****

The air was warm enough for talking, but the students mostly walked in silence to The Mystery of Chocolate. Whether it was the heavy subject matter in tonight's lecture, general fatigue as the term ground to a close, or spring fever, Smyth didn't know. Perhaps there wasn't much left to talk about, or perhaps eating ridiculously rich desserts every Wednesday night had lost its appeal.

Betty convened the formal discussion as usual, but without much enthusiasm. "What do you think about tonight's clue? Anybody?"

The students looked at each other.

"As far as I can see, it doesn't tell us anything we didn't already know," Derek Uluchuk said. "'Roger was not interested in Mary, Alice, or Laura.' So? We already knew that from clue number two. Roger is dating Bev, so of course he's not interested in Mary, Alice, or Laura."

"Maybe it has some hidden significance," Tyler suggested.

"Maybe the professor has run out of useful clues, and he's just filling in with red herrings because he promised to give us a clue every week," Derek countered.

"Maybe the reason nobody has solved his stupid mystery is that he doesn't give out any useful clues," Molly said sullenly. "We still don't know who was murdered, and I don't know why we're even bothering to come here."

The meeting broke up early. Usually Molly, Derek, Brendan, and John Smyth walked back to the campus together, taking the long way around by the street, while the others scattered to their rented rooms and apartments near the shopping district. But tonight Brendan wasn't there, and Derek was headed to the library, which wouldn't close for another hour. So John Smyth walked back the rest of the way alone with Molly, going all the way to the front door of the dorm on the other side of the Riel Building next to the river.

At first they walked in silence, but then Smyth said, "Molly, can I ask you something?"

"Sure. What?"

112

"You don't like Pamela Wright, do you?"

"How do you know?" Molly blurted out.

Smyth smiled. "Well, you and the other girls don't sit with her. You let her sit all alone in the front row."

"I don't think she's looking for girl friends."

"How do you know? Have you asked her?"

"Girls like Pamela don't…"

"Don't what? Don't have girl friends…or don't *want* to have girl friends?"

Molly remained silent for a moment. She turned her head to look at Smyth. "Are you saying this because you think if I became friends with Pamela, she might give me beauty tips?"

"No, I wasn't thinking that at all. I just thought that Pamela could use a friend." He paused. "Do you want to be like Pamela?"

Molly hesitated. "I want to be popular like her."

"That's not the same thing."

They walked in silence the last few hundred feet to the front door of the dorm.

Molly paused on the front steps and tuned to face Smyth. "Thank you for walking back with me," she said. "It made me feel much safer."

Smyth raised one hand and shrugged. "No problem. I'm glad to do it. Good night."

Walking back to his car, Smyth wondered how safe he had made her. She was almost a foot taller than he was and in good condition from her life on the farm. His arms and legs were beginning to ache from his recent snow shoveling. He wondered how safe *he* was as he approached his lonely car in parking lot D, next to the darkened woods of the endowment lands.

# Chapter 27

### Friday, March 20

Devorkian strode into the office. "Finally," he said, and threw a large brown envelope on the desk.

"What's that?" Hosschuk asked.

"Those are student records. Now let's see what's in them." He opened the folder, extracted the sheets and laid the first one on the desk.

### Lorraine Malthus #1009991

| Fall 2010 | Instructor | Grade |
|---|---|---|
| EC100 Introductory Economics I | H.E. Turner | 81 |
| EN100 Introductory English I | Faculty | 74 |
| CO100 Introduction to Business I | R.N. Thoraldson | 82 |
| MT135 Mathematics for Business I | K.J. Chong | 79 |
| PY100 Introductory Psychology I | S.K. Magnusson | 84 |

| Spring 2011 | Instructor | Grade |
|---|---|---|
| EC101 Introductory Economics II | H.E. Turner | 86 |
| EN101 Introductory English II | Faculty | 73 |
| CO101 Introduction to Business II | R.N. Thoraldson | 85 |
| MT136 Mathematics for Business II | K.J. Chong | 76 |
| PY101 Introductory Psychology II | S.K. Magnusson | 87 |

| Fall 2011 | Instructor | Grade |
|---|---|---|
| CO210 Principles of Accounting I | R.A, Martens | 83 |
| CO240 Business Communications | N.A. Misener | 76 |
| CO257 Information Technology | K.L. Lee | 84 |
| CO235 Payroll and Taxation | L.S. Dubrovsky | 91 |
| SO100 Introduction to Sociology I | R.R. Smith, B.K. Janzen | 81 |

| Spring 2012 | Instructor | Grade |
| --- | --- | --- |
| CO211 Principles of Accounting II | R.A, Martens | 83 |
| CO222 Quantitative Decision Making | S.N. Brar | 81 |
| CO257 Organizational Behavior | A.S. Snively | 78 |
| CO237 Employment Law | L.S. Dubrovsky | 85 |
| S0101 Introduction to Sociology II | B.K. Janzen, S.N. Burke | 83 |

| Summer 2012 | Instructor | Grade |
| --- | --- | --- |
| Work Experience | | 85 |

| Fall 2012 | Instructor | Grade |
| --- | --- | --- |
| CO310 Intermediate Accounting I | N.O. Sandhu | 86 |
| CO310 Analyzing Financial Statements | K.N. Windsor | 87 |
| CO333 Collective Agreements | K.O. Mackenzie | 81 |
| PS200 Business and Government | W.R. Waszkowsky | 75 |
| EN225 Classical Literature | P.E. Kingston | 73 |

| Spring 2013 | Instructor | Grade |
| --- | --- | --- |
| CO310 Intermediate Accounting II | N.O. Sandhu | Incomplete |
| CO341 Tax Planning | A.B. Santini | Incomplete |
| CO334 Collective Bargaining | K.O. Mackenzie | Incomplete |
| CO272 Human Resource Management | A.S. Snively | Incomplete |
| HY140 Canadian History I | O.R. Lafleur | Incomplete |

Both men looked over the document.

"Do you see anything significant?" Devorkian asked.

"I don't know. You're the expert in this university stuff. Are those good marks?"

"They demonstrate what was already in our files, that she was a good student but not outstanding. None of the professors' names seems familiar."

"What's this 'Faculty' mean after the English course?"

"It means that in the English Department, the professors take turns teaching first-year English, a lecture or two each, and it sometimes changes, depending on who is available. The university doesn't keep track of who actually teaches in the course, although some of the professors might."

"So that guy with the Malthus theory…"

"Don Henderson."

"Right, Don Henderson. He could have taught Lorraine Malthus first year, and he lied about it because he knows we can't prove whether he did or not."

"Yes, and it's also possible that he taught her but he honestly doesn't remember because he only saw her for one or two lectures, and those first-year classes can be very large."

"The incompletes on her last term," Hosschuk asked. "Do they mean she wasn't doing as well the last term?"

"No. It means she was killed before she wrote her final exams. Sometimes in such cases, the university will issue a mark on the basis of the work done in the course. It's a comfort to the parents."

"And in Lorraine's case, the parents don't care."

"Right. Her father was gone, and she didn't get along with her mother." Devorkian paused. "Shall we move on to the next one?"

### Astrid Andersson #1314031

| Fall 2013 | Instructor | Grade |
|---|---|---|
| SO100 Introduction to Sociology I | R.R. Smith, B.K. Janzen | 72 |
| EN100 Introductory English I | Faculty | 58 |
| AN100 Introduction to Anthropology I | B.L. Saddat | 63 |
| HY140 Canadian History I | O.R. Lafleur | 45 |
| PY100 Introductory Psychology I | S.K. Magnusson | 65 |

| Spring 2014 | Instructor | Grade |
|---|---|---|
| SO101 Introduction to Sociology II | B.K.Janzen, S.N. Burke | Incomplete |
| EN101 Introductory English II | Faculty | Incomplete |
| AN101 Introduction to Anthropology II | B.L. Saddat | Incomplete |
| HY180 American History I | T.O. Leis | Incomplete |
| PY101 Introductory Psychology II | S.K. Magnusson | Incomplete |

"Any ideas about this one?" Devorkian asked.

Hosschuk shrugged. "The marks aren't as good."

"Yes."

"She took introductory English, so she could have met Don Henderson."

"Yes."

"I don't see anything else."

"Neither do I. Here's the next one."

## Meghan Hall #1103451

| Fall 2011 | Instructor | Grade |
| --- | --- | --- |
| SO100 Introduction to Sociology I | R.R. Smith, B.K. Janzen | 91 |
| EN100 Introductory English I | Faculty | 92 |
| FR190 Introduction to French Lit. | F.M. Bergeron | 89 |
| HY140 Canadian History I | O.R. Lafleur | 88 |
| PS100 Introductory Political Science I | J.T. Kingma | 85 |

| Spring 2012 | Instructor | Grade |
| --- | --- | --- |
| SO101 Introduction to Sociology II | B.K. Janzen, S.N. Burke | 93 |
| EN101 Introductory English II | Faculty | 94 |
| FR170 Introduction to Québécois Lit. | J.P. LaSalle | 85 |
| HY141 Canadian History II | K.O. Marshall | 86 |
| PS101 Introductory Political Science II | J.T. Kingma | 84 |

| Fall 2012 | Instructor | Grade |
| --- | --- | --- |
| EN211 Shakespeare's Plays | B.O. Young | 91 |
| EN280 American Literature I | B.L. McGwire | 95 |
| EN250 Romantic Poetry | D.H. Henderson | 89 |
| EC100 Introductory Economics I | H.E. Turner | 84 |
| EN138 Creative Writing | T.N. Hanna | 92 |

| Spring 2013 | Instructor | Grade |
| --- | --- | --- |
| EN212 Elizabethan/Jacobean Poetry | B.O. Young | 90 |
| EN281 American Literature II | D.R. Hemenhof | 91 |
| EN251 Victorian Poetry | D.H. Henderson | 92 |
| EC100 Introductory Economics II | H.E. Turner | 83 |
| EN292 Principles of Copyediting | J.S. Hardy-Miller | 89 |

| Fall 2013 | Instructor | Grade |
| --- | --- | --- |
| EN380 Canadian Literature I | B.B. Bodkowsky | 91 |
| EN350 The Victorian Novel | D.N. Nickerson | 91 |
| EN225 Classical Literature | P.E. Kingston | 80 |
| EN391 Writing Poetry | T.N. Hanna | 92 |
| HY257 European Thought 1689-1914 | N.Y. Mason | 89 |

| Spring 2014 | Instructor | Grade |
| --- | --- | --- |
| EN381 Canadian Literature II | B.B. Bodkowsky | 93 |
| EN341 The Mystery Novel | D.R. Hemenhof | 82 |
| EN325 The Birth of the Novel | D.N. Nickerson | 91 |
| HY241 The Protestant Reformation | J.B. Witherspoon | 85 |
| PL100 Introduction to Philosophy | J.D. Manuel | 96 |

"Meghan's marks are certainly higher," Hosschuk said without being asked.

"Those are very good marks, exceptional marks, in fact," Devorkian agreed. "Anything else?"

"She took two courses from Don Henderson, not counting first-year English."

"Right, but we already knew that. And first-year English appears to be the only course overlapping with the other victims'."

Hosschuk was silent.

"And the HY257 course is the one that is likely to have included the Malthusian theory," Devorkian said.

"There are no incompletes. So that means her parents asked that she get that...credit..."

"Maybe. But she was killed almost two weeks later. She had probably written most of her final exams."

They were silent for several moments.

"There is one more," Devorkian said.

### David Horcoff #1209657

| Fall 2012 | Instructor | Grade |
| --- | --- | --- |
| SO100 Introduction to Sociology I | R.R. Smith, B.K. Janzen | 90 |
| EN100 Introductory English I | Faculty | 93 |
| HY140 Canadian History I | O.R. Lafleur | 85 |
| PS100 Introductory Political Science I | J.T. Kingma | 84 |
| EN138 Creative Writing | T.N. Hanna | 95 |

| Spring 2013 | Instructor | Grade |
| --- | --- | --- |
| SO101 Introduction to Sociology II | B.K. Janzen, S.N. Burke | 89 |
| EN101 Introductory English II | Faculty | 92 |
| HY141 Canadian History II | K.O. Marshall | 89 |
| PS101 Introductory Political Science II | J.T. Kingma | 88 |

| DR167 Introduction to Film | S.V. Epstein | 90 |

| Fall 2013 | Instructor | Grade |
| --- | --- | --- |
| EN211 Shakespeare's Plays | B.O. Young | 88 |
| EN280 American Literature I | B.L. McGwire | 94 |
| EN225 Classical Literature | P.E. Kingston | 88 |
| PY100 Introductory Psychology I | S.K. Magnusson | 85 |
| HY257 European Thought 1689-1914 | N.Y. Mason | 87 |

| Spring 2014 | Instructor | Grade |
| --- | --- | --- |
| EN212 Elizabethan/Jacobean Poetry | B.O. Young | 88 |
| EN281 American Literature II | D.R. Hemenhof | 91 |
| EN293 Writing the Short Story | T.N. Hanna | 95 |
| EN267 Essential Script Writing | B.N. McIntyre | 94 |
| PY100 Introductory Psychology II | S.K. Magnusson | 87 |

| Fall 2014 | Instructor | Grade |
| --- | --- | --- |
| EN380 Canadian Literature I | B.B. Bodkowsky | 90 |
| EN350 The Victorian Novel | D.N. Nickerson | 89 |
| EN385 The Modern American Novel | J.T. Montgomery | 90 |
| EN391 Writing Poetry | T.N. Hanna | 97 |
| PS257 Social Change in Canadian Politics | S.R. Hartsburg | 87 |

| Spring 2015 | Instructor | Grade |
| --- | --- | --- |
| EN381 Canadian Literature II | B.B. Bodkowsky | Incomplete |
| EN341 The Mystery Novel | D.R. Hemenhof | Incomplete |
| EN325 The Birth of the Novel | D.N. Nickerson | Incomplete |
| EN393 Plot and Characterization | J.M. Howe | Incomplete |
| RE161 Introduction to Christianity | S.V. Michaelson | Incomplete |

"You got Horcoff's list?" Hosschuk asked.

"It took some paperwork, but yes," Devorkian answered. "What do you see?"

"He's got good marks."

"And he's taking a lot of the same courses Meghan took. That may explain why she was going out with him. They had a lot in common."

Hosschuk put the two sheets together. "And they took the Creative Writing course at the same time—and that history course that includes that Malthus theory."

"Horcoff was a year behind Meghan, so he took a lot of the same courses a year after her, as if he was following in her footsteps," Devorkian said. He pulled another sheet over. "And he took psychology at the same time as Astrid Andersson. It seems he left a few things out."

"But he told us he knew Astrid, didn't he?"

"He said he met her in the pub. Of course, psychology's a big class. He might not remember her from there."

"Didn't the counseling records say she skipped class sometimes?"

"Universities don't keep records of attendance, but that's certainly a possibility judging from her marks."

"So we can connect him to two of the victims. But we can't connect him to Lorraine Malthus," Hosschuk said.

"She was the first one."

"You mean maybe the first time he killed a stranger and then later killed two people he did know? Isn't that unusual? Don't serial killers usually start with someone they know?"

"Yes. But he did take the course on the other Malthus."

"That was afterwards."

# Chapter 28
## Wednesday, March 25

The kids had been slow, the puddles from the melting snow had been deep, the traffic had been heavy, and Smyth had been tired. Rushing around the bend in the hall, he collided head on with the janitor, a man six inches taller, sixty pounds heavier and five years younger. The younger man grabbed Smyth in a powerful hand to keep him from falling.

"I'm terribly sorry," Smyth stammered. "I'm late, and I didn't see you, and the teacher already doesn't like me, and…" He realized he was babbling.

He hurried into the room and slid into the seat beside Derek Uluchuk.

"This is not the class in which you want to be described as the late Mr. Smyth." Vintage Hitchcock, delivered with an exaggerated deadpan, Hemenhof's ad lib drew a burst of laughter from the students.

"Today," Hemenhof continued in the same voice, "we will talk about the hero in mystery novels. There was a time when mysteries seemed to be an extension of morality plays, a contest between good and evil in which the good hero discovered and punished the evil murderer. Thankfully, those days are gone. Today's mysteries are far more nuanced and realistic. They show people with different personalities, different problems, and different abilities interacting. There is a central character with whom we identify, but there are no good and bad people, there is no good and evil. In G.M. Ford's *Black River,* for instance, the hero murders two hit men and then pins a murder they didn't commit on them. The hero comments, 'It was much more ambiguous than I figured. It was hard to tell the good guys from the bad guys. There didn't seem to be any moral high ground. More like we all just got down in the swamp together and rolled around in the muck.' That is what a modern mystery is like, and it is far more realistic. Modern mysteries have discarded the archaic concepts of good and evil."

Hemenhof suddenly turned. "Okay, Mr. Smyth, you can raise your objection now."

Smyth stammered, "I, uh, wasn't going to object."

"No?'

"No. I agree with you. I think you're right that perfectly good heroes battling completely evil bad guys isn't very realistic. And I also think you're right that the heroes in modern mysteries often aren't any better than the criminals."

"Good." Hemenhof straightened. "Maybe I'm finally getting through to you."

"But I still believe in good and evil," Smyth said in a small voice.

"What?"

"I don't think the battle between good and evil is as much a battle between good and evil people as it is a battle between good and evil within each human being. Human beings are sinful."

"Sinful is not a word we use in this class, Mr. Smyth. This is a literature course, not a theology course."

"People do evil things then, but I also believe that some people are more evil than others, and that the hero in a murder mystery should be less evil than the murderer."

Hemenhof came close to Smyth, bent over and spoke very slowly as if he was speaking to someone mentally deficient. "Modern mysteries aren't like that."

"I know," Smyth said, "but they should be. Sherlock Holmes had problems with depression and with opium, but he was still morally better than the criminals he was chasing. I don't like modern mysteries as much because I have trouble identifying with the heroes. If the hero in a mystery novel is just as bad as the criminals, then why don't we root for the criminal, why would we care if the criminal is caught? Why would we read those books?"

"But people do read those books, Mr. Smyth. They read them because the books reflect what the world is really like."

"I already know what the world is like. That's why I want to change it."

"People like you don't change the world, Mr. Smyth."

Molly Pembroke raised her hand. "One of the things that bothers me in some of the newer books on the reading list," she said, "is that the heroes treat everyone around them with contempt because they are smarter and stronger than everyone else. Sherlock Holmes and Hercule Poirot were smarter than other people, but they still treated them with respect and compassion."

"Miss Pembroke, how brave of you to contribute to the discussion," Hemenhof said, turning in her direction. "You are right. That is how Sherlock Holmes and Hercule Poirot treated people. But it's not very realistic."

"Really?" Smyth asked. "Hasn't anyone ever treated you with compassion?"

"They don't need to because I'm obviously smarter than those around me." Hemenhof raised his eyebrows.

The class snickered.

Hemenhof continued, "It seems to me, Mr. Smyth, that you have been reading Clive Staple's book."

"Well, yes I have," Smyth stammered. "After you recommended it the other week…"

"I did not recommend it," Hemenhof said.

"Oh," Smyth finished in a small voice.

*****

"We're finally getting somewhere," Betty Borden declared to the group around the table. Only two of them had desserts. The novelty of The Mystery of Chocolate was wearing off, and money was getting tight for some of the students as the term drew to a close.

"Right," Derek answered. "Week eleven, and he finally told us who was murdered."

"I thought Professor Hemenhof said that the murder was supposed to take place at the beginning of a book," Molly said.

"Yes, but this isn't a book," Betty answered. "He said you put the murder at the beginning of a book so people will be interested and read the book. But this is an assignment, so he doesn't have to do anything to make us interested. We have to do it whether we're interested or not."

"But we have been interested," Derek said. "The murder doesn't have to come at the beginning of the book if other things in the book interest us enough. I think that's one of the reasons Professor Hemenhof gave us this assignment—to teach us what makes a mystery work."

"That's good," Molly said. "Write that down, Betty. It should go in our report. We could get some extra marks for that."

"Okay," Betty said, making a note. "Now, what specifically does this clue tell us: 'He killed Laura partly because he wanted to try everything, and he wondered what it would be like to kill someone'?"

"That's easy," Derek said. "We know who the victim is, Laura. And it was one of the four guys. We know it wasn't Larry because he thought his brother did it. That leaves Roger, Rob, and Harry. But we know neither Roger nor Rob is Larry's brother, so it has to be Harry."

"It's probably Harry, but I don't think we have absolute proof yet," Betty said.

"No, but we're pretty close," Derek said.

# Chapter 29

*Friday, March 27*

"It's finally all approved," Devorkian enthused. "The lights go up tomorrow."

"What lights?" Hosschuk asked. "I thought we were working on this case together. You've been doing something you didn't tell me about."

"You're a sergeant. I'm a detective," Devorkian said. "You tell me everything you know. I tell you what you need to hear." He took a deep breath. "I've been working on this for three months."

"Working on what?"

"We're putting in new lights in university parking lot D next to the endowment lands."

"Extra lights? It took you three months to get new lights installed in a parking lot?"

"You have to understand how universities operate. The plan had to be approved by the university governing board, and the board wouldn't approve it until the issue had been studied by a committee with representatives from the administration, faculty, and student body. We finally got approval last night, and the lights are being installed on Saturday."

"So the students knew about this, and I didn't."

"A couple of the students knew because they had to know. I've been trying to keep this project as secret as possible."

"Why? Everyone's going to know about the lights as soon as they're installed. And how much difference is extra lighting going to make anyway?"

"Ah, but these are special lights." Devorkian smiled. "The lights have miniature cameras embedded in them. We're going to keep all sides of the endowment lands under surveillance."

"All sides?"

"Sure. The supermarket at the other end of the endowment lands already has surveillance cameras. They're essential security equipment nowadays. Everybody has them."

"Everybody but the university."

"Yes. And the supermarket manager agreed we could look at the tapes the day I asked him three months ago."

"Then why did it take the university so long?"

"The university is concerned that we do not invade the privacy of its students and faculty."

"Even if it means some of them get murdered and we never catch the killer?"

"Precisely." Devorkian frowned. "We had to agree to certain... limitations."

"What sort of limitations?"

"The cameras are approved for a one-month trial period, and the videotapes are on a continuous loop so we are only allowed to keep records for a twenty-four-hour period."

"Oh."

"And because the cameras are on the lights at the top of the poles pointing down, we're not going to get a great look at faces."

"So the cameras might not be that useful."

"They're the best hope we have right now."

"But they'll only be on for a month."

"The first two murders were committed on the weekend after classes ended and before the final exams began. That's a week from now."

Hosschuk was silent. "You realize that the cameras might help us catch the killer, but they probably won't stop him from killing again, especially if he kills the victim somewhere else and just uses the woods to dump her body?"

"I'm aware of that. But it's better than letting him kill ten more times. And starting on Friday evening a week from now, we are going to have undercover officers hidden all around the endowment lands. Then, when we see anything suspicious, we may be able to intervene in time to save a life."

"What if the killer finds out we're watching and kills somewhere else?"

"That's why I'm trying to keep this from being known."

"But some students know. What's to keep them from passing the information on?"

"They were given the information in confidence."

"What's to keep them from passing the information on?"

"I know. It's a problem. We just have to hope they don't pass it on to the wrong person."

"Do you really think he will kill again?"

"There's a pattern. He's done it two years in a row. My instincts say he will try again."

# Chapter 30

## Sunday, March 29

A powerful hand gripped his shoulder, pinning Smyth in his place. He looked up to see Don Henderson, almost a foot taller, looking down at him. He felt like a child next to people like Henderson. Sometimes the "close fellowship" at Central Grace Evangelical Church seemed to him a little too close.

"How's it going, John?" Henderson asked.

"Okay."

"How is the course going?"

Smyth sighed. "I feel like I've been through a war."

Henderson laughed. "I feel like that just about every day. The question is: Are you winning the war?"

"I don't know. I am almost finished the major paper. It's due at the final class a week from Wednesday. I'm fairly happy with the paper, but with Professor Hemenhof I just don't know what he's thinking. I don't know if I am going to pass the course or not."

"Of course, you're going to pass, John. You've got Meghan's notes, remember?" Sheila Hall had come up on the other side of him."

Smyth jumped. "Oh, hi, Sheila. Yes, Meghan's notes are very thorough and well organized. I think they're going to be a great help when I study for the final exam."

"Better than those chicken scratchings of yours, eh, John?" Henderson said. He finally released his grip on Smyth's shoulders. "Let me know if there's anything I can do to help you."

"Thanks, Don. I'll do that. Thank you too, Sheila." Smyth looked up to see Ruby halfway across the church foyer, smiling at his predicament. "If you'll excuse me, I need to gather up the kids and get home for dinner."

# Chapter 31

## Wednesday, April 1

John Smyth was on time this night and did not collide with the janitor in the hallway. He was sitting in the third row next to Derek Uluchuk when he noticed Molly Pembroke come in. She glanced at Smyth, smiled, and then purposefully walked over and sat down next to Pamela Wright in the front row. They talked quietly, intermittently, and stiffly at first, then with a little more animation. A few moments later, Betty Borden came in. She glanced around the room and then, with a puzzled look on her face, focused on Molly. Molly raised a hand, and Betty walked over and sat beside Molly.

"We have got to stop meeting like this."

Smyth, watching the three young women, had not noticed Hemenhof come in.

Hemenhof opened a book and began reading out loud, dramatically. It was a description of violent, raunchy sex. "That is how Slade Coulter opens his novel *Red Raw Alley*. Think about how Agatha Christie opens her novels, with a group of refined upper-class gentlemen and ladies having tea. It was an artificial construct, a genteel society that never existed. Today's fiction is more realistic. It presents life as it is, with all of its ugly, confused, and violent edges hanging out." He paused. "Mr. Smyth, what is it now?"

Smyth couldn't help himself. "The characters in Mr. Coulter's books have multiple sexual partners, drink excessively, take drugs, and are always getting into fights."

"Yes, Mr. Smyth. It's reality. Get used to it."

"But the back cover of the book says that Mr. Coulter lives on Saltspring Island with his wife and two children. Most of us don't live the way the characters in his books do, and neither does Mr. Coulter."

\*\*\*\*\*

Winter is long in Winnipeg, but spring is short. In February, everything is still frozen solid. By April, the temperature can rise to thirty degrees Celsius, the high eighties Fahrenheit. By the beginning of April this year, the snow had been melting for two weeks. There was already flooding in the outlying areas, and there was talk that the gates of the floodway might be opened. The floodway is a great ditch around the city, a manmade moat thirty feet deep, a thousand feet wide and twenty-nine miles long that in flood years diverts excess water from the Red River and saves Winnipeg itself from flooding. Spring was in the air, and Winnipeggers were moving with a lightness and joy now that the heavy oppression of winter seemed to finally be lifting.

The sidewalks were free of snow, and the students could walk three abreast. Molly Pembroke fell in beside John Smyth and Derek Uluchuk. "Go walk with Betty," she said to Derek. "I want to talk with Mr. Smyth."

"Got a thing for the old man, eh?" Derek caught up to Betty and with a show of mock gallantry offered her his arm. Betty laughed and took it. It was spring.

Smyth and Molly walked in silence for a while.

"You talked to Pamela," Smyth said.

"Yes."

"How was it?"

"She was...nice. She was friendly."

"Good."

"And kind of sad."

"You didn't expect that?"

"No."

"Did you invite her to the discussion?"

"Yes. She said she would like to come but she had a date."

"Who with?"

"Don Hamilton."

"Did she say that?"

"No, she wouldn't say at first, so I asked if it was Don Hamilton, and she smiled and laughed."

"Do you mind that?"

Molly was silent a moment. "Yes. I'm closer to Don's height, and I'm athletic like he is." She sighed. "But I don't want him if he's not interested in me."

"How are you doing?"

"I'm okay. I'm going to pass all my courses…and it's spring!"

They had arrived at The Mystery of Chocolate. When they were sitting around the table, Betty as usual opened the discussion. "Tonight's clue confirms that we were on the right track." She read from her notes, "'Larry was right although he didn't guess the whole story.' That refers to clue number nine, where Larry thought his brother had done it because of jealousy."

"Okay," Derek said, "but what does it mean that Larry didn't understand the whole picture?"

"It means that Larry thought he did it because of jealousy, but, according to clue number eleven, he also did it because he wanted to experience what it was like to kill someone."

"So, we've got it solved," Betty said. "Should I write it up and hand it in?"

There was silence.

"Sure," Molly said. "It would be great if you did that."

"Okay," Betty answered. "But can all of you lend me any notes you've made on this, either on paper or by email?"

Some of the group handed over notes, and others wrote down Betty's email address.

"Maybe, just to be safe, before you hand it in, we should wait for the final clue," Derek said. "It might give us more marks if we include that in our argument."

"You just want to have an excuse to come back here one more week," Molly teased.

"Why are you in such a good mood today?" Derek asked.

"Because it's spring," she answered. Then she became more serious. "And because I learned something in this course. Harry killed Laura because of jealousy. It made me realize how deadly jealousy is. It kills people."

John Smyth smiled.

# Chapter 32
## *Wednesday, April 8*

Smyth was surprised to see Don Henderson again on Wednesday, walking into the Riel Building as Smyth parked his old gray station wagon in parking lot D. When he got inside, Henderson was nowhere to be seen. There was just the janitor methodically vacuuming the hall. Henderson had probably gone up to his office on the second floor. It was odd. Smyth didn't recall seeing Henderson at the university in the evening before. He was a very methodical and predictable man. Smyth entered the classroom and sat, as usual, beside Derek Uluchuk.

"It is no accident," Professor Hemenhof said, "that the mystery novel only began to be written in the nineteenth century. Before that time, there were only rudimentary police forces and certainly no specially trained detectives. Until that time, a criminal investigation mostly consisted of authorities offering a reward and asking anyone who might have witnessed anything to come forward. But even after the creation of police forces, methods of investigation had hardly moved forward very much.

"Consider Agatha Christie's Miss Marple. This is a woman who has only a general idea about the evidence. How then does she solve murders? She solves murders because she knows people. In explaining how she solved a particular case, she usually says, 'Well, my dear, the criminal reminded me of Mr. Williamson, the butcher, from back home in the village of St. Mary Mead.'" Here Hemenhof spoke in a high, spinsterish whisper.

"Technology has changed all that. The first major breakthrough was the discovery and classification of fingerprints in the nineteenth century. But fingerprints weren't commonly used in criminal investigations until the second half of the twentieth century. This was followed by ballistics, in which experts examine the unique marks left on bullets by gun barrels. The next most significant advance was the discovery of DNA in the last twenty years or so. This has allowed investigators to determine the identity of criminals from semen or hair follicles found at the scene of a crime. But these are only the two most obvious elements in a vast technological revolution that has changed criminal investigation forever. Crimes are now solved by experts examining the chemical composition of cloth fragments, the physics of blood spatter, the unique pattern of car tire treads. All of these innovations have been popularized by the TV show *CSI*. Technological innovations have not only changed the nature of criminal investigations but also the nature of mystery stories. Mystery writers cannot ignore what their readers have learned from *CSI*. If they write in the old way, their readers are going to undermine their books with technological questions. Why didn't the police check his DNA? Why didn't they analyze the woman's perfume? Why didn't someone call the police on a cell phone? Older mysteries involved the careful study of people. Modern mysteries focus on the careful study of evidence."

Hemenhof turned to John Smyth. "Well, Mr. Smyth, aren't you going to question me?"

"No," Smyth answered. "I think you're right. But to some extent, I am sorry about the change, at least for mystery novels. I find people far more interesting and important than science."

"It's not about your personal preferences, Mr. Smyth. It's about reality." He paused and smiled. "It's been great having you in the class, Mr. Smyth. You ask all the obvious questions and raise all the naïve objections. You're not afraid to make a fool of yourself by giving wrong answers. You have been a wonderful teaching tool."

Almost three hours later, Hemenhof finished his lecture and stopped. "We have reached the place in the course," he said, "when a good sleuth would have figured out the solutions. Do you know the answers? Have you figured out the mystery novel? The concluding chapter will come two weeks from tonight when you write the final exam. It's been enjoyable teaching you this term."

The class applauded him on cue.

"Any final questions?" he asked.

Betty Borden raised her hand. "You haven't given us the final clue to the second assignment."

"Right," Hemenhof answered. "Remember that your research papers are due tonight. So far, I haven't received any answers to the second assignment. You can still hand in the answers anytime leading up to the final exam. I am in my office most days and even many evenings. Call me on my cell phone or just drop in and give me your answers. It is fitting that the course end with the revelation of the final clue. Here it is." He paused dramatically. "None of the men had an alibi...except Harry."

The students sat for a moment in stunned silence and then began gathering up their books and filing out. The group of seven met in parking lot D.

"Shall we bother to go tonight?" Betty asked.

"Why not?" Derek answered. "Let's finish the class off with a party!"

"Sure," Smyth said. "I'll buy a whole cake we can divide."

"Are you sure Mrs. Smyth is okay with this?" Derek asked.

"Yes. It was her idea."

They had reached the edge of the parking lot. "Smile for the cameras," Tyler Tapinski said. "Big brother is watching."

"What are you talking about?" Betty asked.

"The police department has installed video cameras on the poles in the parking lot."

"Why?" Betty asked.

"Because they want to spy on innocent students minding their own business."

"How do you know about this?" Molly asked.

"Because the university set up a committee to decide whether to let the police do it. As student body president, I was on the committee."

"I didn't know you were president," Smyth said.

Tyler shrugged.

"I take it the committee approved the installation?" Smyth asked.

"Yes, but I voted against it."

"Are you sure you're supposed to be telling us this?" Smyth asked.

"They told us not to tell anyone, but police states always say that so no one finds out what they're doing. Information is power, and power belongs to the people."

"Does this have anything to do with the students who were murdered in the endowment lands the last two years?" Smyth asked.

"That's what they said, but I think they just want to spy on students. It's an unjustified invasion of privacy."

"Well, I feel safer knowing they're there," Molly said.

"You won't when the storm troopers come to get you," Tyler answered.

They walked on mostly in silence through the warm evening.

When they were seated around the table at The Mystery of Chocolate with the triple chocolate fudge cake sitting in front of them, Smyth said, "I want to thank you for letting me be part of the group, for accepting me. It makes me feel young again."

"Hey, we accept you," Derek said. "But you're still old."

The others laughed.

When they had finished eating, Betty said, "Okay, shall we discuss tonight's clue?"

"Let's not," Derek said.

"We thought we had it figured out, but if Harry didn't do it, everything we decided must be wrong," Molly complained. "No wonder no one ever figures this out. I don't think there is a solution."

"There must be," Smyth said. "There must be another solution we're not thinking of."

"Sure, but what?" Derek asked.

Nobody said anything.

Betty pulled some sheets of paper out of her backpack. "This is what I wrote up last week," Betty said. "I think I included everything we talked about. And I put on the names of everyone who came even once."

"Even the old man's wife?" Derek asked.

Everyone laughed. Then there was silence as they all read over the summary.

Derek shrugged. "Looks good."

"But is there any point handing it in?" Betty asked.

"Sure," Molly said. "You have to hand it in. We'll still get a mark for completing the assignment, just no bonus marks for solving it."

"Okay, I'll add a paragraph about tonight's clue and hand it in," Betty said, standing up. "Thank you for the cake, Mr. Smyth. Come on, Molly."

Smyth looked puzzled.

"Betty invited me to stay at her place tonight," Molly explained. "The kids in the dorm get crazy at the end of the term, and sometimes it's hard to sleep."

Smyth began gathering up the remnants of the cake to take back to Ruby and the kids. The others were heading for the door, but David Horcoff remained sitting.

"Are you coming, David?" Smyth asked.

David shook his head.

Smyth sat back down.

"Do you believe what Meghan believed, Mr. Smyth?" David asked. "That stuff about God."

"I don't know exactly what Meghan told you, but yes, David, I do believe what Meghan believed."

"I don't."

"That doesn't mean it's not true."

"I don't believe God cares what we do, and he isn't going to punish us for doing what you think is wrong. I agree with Professor Hemenhof. God doesn't exist, and there is no such thing as good and evil."

Smyth absorbed this information. "Then why does the question still bother you? Maybe you just don't want to believe, or are afraid to."

David said nothing more and dismissed Smyth with a wave of his hand.

Smyth gathered up his cake and his briefcase and said, "Good night, David. I hope you find the right answers to your questions." He headed toward the door, then stopped and came back. "David," he said.

The younger man looked up.

"Just over a year ago, your friend Meghan Hall was murdered," Smyth said. "If you say there is no such thing as morality, then you're saying it was okay for somebody to squeeze the life out of her and discard her body in the endowment lands. There is such a thing as evil, and that is an example of it."

Smyth turned then and went out the door. Brendan, Tyler, and Derek were already two blocks ahead of him, heading toward campus. He would have to walk back to parking lot D alone. When the dark tangle of the endowment lands loomed out of the darkness on his right, he shivered. With relief, he rounded the corner of the woods and reached the parking lot. Another car pulled out as he neared his own.

Unconsciously, he smiled up at the cameras. The Riel Building stood like a dark fortress on the far side of the parking lot. Three or four windows still showed light, and he wondered who was still working this late. It was just after eleven. Perhaps it was only the janitor finishing his cleaning.

# Chapter 33

## *Thursday, April 9*

Molly Pembroke said she was athletic. She was tall and strong, but she was not agile. It was eight forty-five in the morning, and she was rushing along the paved path through the endowment lands, anxious to be on time for a nine o'clock class. Her foot caught on a portion of pavement raised by a tree root, and she fell headlong. Her first reaction was the normal one of acute embarrassment, but as she turned to see what it was that had tripped her—it couldn't be her own clumsiness that was at fault—she caught a glimpse of something in the underbrush. That glimpse froze her upward movement, and she bent again for a closer look. In a second, she was on her feet. Two young women were walking toward her.

"Are you okay?" One of them asked the usual, mindless question.

Molly answered the question with one of her own. "Do you have a cell phone?"

"What?"

"Do you have a cell phone?"

"Yes."

"Give it to me."

The other woman, just over five feet tall, stared up at Molly's nearly six feet of height and silently, fumblingly handed over the instrument. Molly grabbed it and quickly punched in three numbers.

*****

Hosschuk was sitting at his desk when Devorkian breezed by, grabbing him by the shoulder. "Let's go," he said. "He's early."

They flew through the end of the rush hour, the siren wailing a lament, and pulled up in the mall parking lot next to the endowment lands. Devorkian swore and pulled out his cell phone. "Get a cherry picker down to the university and change those tapes," he barked, then punched the off button.

There were three other police cars in the lot, and the woods were blocked off with yellow tape. Devorkian also noted two minivans and a panel truck. He and Hosschuk ducked under the tape and walked toward a knot of people about two hundred yards along the paved path into the endowment lands. Most of them were standing on the pavement, but three had moved into the bush to the right. The others moved aside, allowing Devorkian to approach a series of dense bushes about six feet high. He knelt and peered underneath.

The first thing he saw was a pair of bare feet. Beyond them was a splash of bright red. A squatting figure to the left of the body said, "Good morning, Alexander. Do you want to see?"

Devorkian shook his head. "No, thanks, Abner. I'll wait till you're done." He stood up and straightened his back. He and Hosschuk stood on the path with the others, watching intently and waiting.

A few minutes later, a round figure in a rumpled brown business suit pushed through the bushes to the left of the body. He looked up at Devorkian. "There is a slight gap here, which the forensics guys say the killer may have used. They found some indications of shoeprints, but nothing useable, so they say it is okay for us to use it." He pushed back through the bushes, and Devorkian and Hosschuk followed, being careful to disturb the soil and the undergrowth as little as possible.

She was of less than average height and lying on her back. Blonde hair, slightly askew, framed a heavily made-up face. She was dressed in a short red party dress hiked up to her hips, revealing lacy black panties. Her legs and feet were bare. Beside her lay a long leather coat and an oversized leather handbag. Her throat was bruised.

"She was strangled?" Devorkian asked.

The man in the rumpled suit nodded. "It appears so."

"Was she killed here?"

The rumpled figure shrugged. "She was placed in that position, on her back, shortly after death, but she may have been moved after that, and I can't say she was killed here."

"Time of death?"

"My best guess is about ten hours ago. It partly depends on how cool it was last night."

Devorkian looked at his watch. It was a little after ten a.m. "Was she sexually assaulted?"

The rumpled man shook his head. "Anything more will have to wait until after the autopsy."

"Okay." Devorkian straightened. "As far as I'm concerned, you can move the body."

They pushed their way back through the brush. Devorkian approached another officer in a white suit. "Crassner, let me know as soon as you get to that leather bag. I want an ID as soon as possible."

The officer nodded.

"Do we know who found the body?"

The man nodded toward the opposite end of the main path through the endowment lands. "I think they took her to the university parking lot."

"That's where I'll be then," Devorkian replied. "What do you think?" he asked, as he and Hosschuk headed down the path.

"It looks like the work of the same man." Hosschuk paused a moment. "Why did you say he was early?"

"Because the first two years the victims were killed on the weekend after classes had ended. This year, classes continue until tomorrow."

"Do you think that is significant?"

"I don't know. If he is starting early, maybe he plans to kill more this year."

"You mean our theory that he might escalate—one the first year, two the second year, and three this year?"

"Perhaps. But it also means we weren't ready. Our full surveillance wasn't scheduled to start until tomorrow night."

"It doesn't look as if he went to a lot of effort to hide the body," Hosschuk offered.

"No. She was just dumped into the bushes. But still she was hidden well enough that she might not have been found for several days, long enough for the evidence to become muddled. We were lucky there."

"We have a good estimate of the time of death, you mean?"

"That, and nothing seems to have got at the body. It hasn't rained. And we're still within the twenty-four hours on the camera tape loop. We will have tape of the time she was killed and dumped."

They had come out into parking lot D, the paved expanse between the campus and the endowment lands. The east side of the lot toward the woods had been cordoned off in yellow tape, and there were a variety of police vehicles parked within it.

The sun was shining brightly, and it promised to be a beautiful spring day with a high temperature of ten to twelve degrees Celsius, halfway between freezing and room temperature. Winnipeggers, acclimatized to the winter, would be walking around without gloves or hats, with their spring coats unbuttoned, rejoicing in the balmy conditions.

Devorkian and Hosschuk approached one of the police cruisers; a young woman was sitting in the back, with the door ajar. Even sitting, the detectives could tell she was tall. She had long brown hair and even features, but her face was too broad to be called pretty.

Devorkian pulled open the other rear door and got in beside her. Hosschuk moved to the front passenger seat. The young woman was clutching a cup of coffee like a teddy bear, and her eyes looked haunted.

Devorkian offered his most reassuring smile. "I'm Detective Devorkian. I understand you are the one who…called us."

The girl nodded.

"What's your name?"

"Molly Pembroke. I showed my driver's license to the other officer, and he wrote it down."

"Can you tell me about it?"

"I was in a hurry to get to class, and I tripped. The path is uneven. As I got up, I turned my head a bit, I saw under the bushes, and there was…" She trailed off.

"Was anyone with you?"

Molly shook her head. "But there were some other girls, and I borrowed a cell phone."

"Do you know these other girls?"

Molly shook her head.

"You waited for the police, but they didn't?"

"They said they had a class."

"Your actions have been very responsible and very helpful," Devorkian said. "Now this is important. Did you go to take a closer look at the young woman in the bushes?"

Molly shook her head.

"Did the other girls?"

Another shake. "They didn't want to…I'm not sure they believed me when I said there was…"

"You thought right away that the young woman was dead?"

Molly nodded. "She looked so…cold and still…And I remembered the other girls…from the other years…"

Devorkian nodded.

"Is she dead?" Molly blurted anxiously.

"I'm afraid so, Molly," Devorkian said reassuringly. "She has been dead for hours. There was nothing you could have done for her."

"Is it Pamela?"

Devorkian stiffened. "You know her?"

"I don't know. I thought it might be Pamela Wright. It looked like her dress…"

"Who's Pamela Wright?"

"Another student. She's in my English class."

"Do you know her well?"

"No. I only talked to her a couple of times. Mr. Smyth suggested I should talk to her."

"Who's Mr. Smith?"

"He's an older man, but he's taking the class too."

"Why did he suggest you talk to Pamela?"

"I think he thought she might be lonely and needed a friend."

"How did he know that? Had he talked to her?"

"I don't think so. He just seems observant. He's older, you know."

"Wiser?"

"Yeah, maybe."

"So what did you learn about Pamela?"

"Not a lot. We only talked a couple of times. Mr. Smyth was right. She did seem lonely—and kind of sad. I invited her to our study group."

"What kind of study group?"

"A bunch of us get together every week after our English class to work on a project."

"Did she join you?"

"No. She thanked me but said she had a date every Wednesday evening."

"The class met on Wednesday evenings?"

"Yes, every Wednesday from seven to ten."

"That was last night?"

Molly nodded.

"Who did Pamela have a date with on Wednesday evenings?"

"I don't know. We guessed it might be Don Hamilton. He's on the university football team, and he's in the class too."

"Why did you think it might be Don Hamilton?"

"I'm not sure. He's good looking, and she was too. And he didn't come to our study group either."

"What's the name of the class?"

"English 341. It's about mystery novels, detective stories."

Devorkian heard a noise and looked up. A gurney carrying a black bag was being wheeled into the parking lot from the endowment lands, toward the open doors of a black van.

"Molly, I know this is a lot to ask, but would you be willing to look at the body and tell us if it's Pamela? It would help us a lot."

Molly nodded. "I don't want to look, but it's better than not knowing."

"Hold up there," Devorkian called to the men with the gurney as he climbed out of the cruiser.

Molly got out and approached the gurney much more slowly and tentatively. She took a deep breath, and one of the men unzipped the black bag enough to reveal a distorted face framed by blonde hair.

Molly gasped and began to cry. "Yes, it's Pamela."

Devorkian motioned to the men to zip up the bag. He did not offer Molly a shoulder to cry on but pulled a spotless white linen handkerchief from the breast pocket of his suit coat and handed it to her. "Molly, you have been very helpful. I am sorry you had to go through this. Is there anyone you would like us to call for you?"

Molly shook her head. "No, thanks. I think I'll go back to the dorm and phone my parents—and maybe some friends."

"You live in the dorm?"

Molly nodded.

"Then why were you walking through the endowment lands this morning?"

"I stayed with a friend last night."

Devorkian smiled.

"A female friend."

Devorkian continued smiling.

Molly turned and walked away. As she went, Devorkian said to Hosschuk, "I wonder who this friend was."

Hosschuk smiled.

At that moment, a cherry picker, a truck with a boom on it, pulled into the parking lot. Both men watched it speculatively for a moment.

"Let's hope those cameras show us something," Devorkian said.

Hosschuk nodded. "So what's next?"

"I want you to go down to the supermarket at the other end of the endowment lands and get their surveillance tapes. See if you can find any other cameras on stores near there or along the road beside the endowment lands.

"Right. What are you going to be doing?"

"I'm going to try to convince the university administration to give me a list of students in that mystery novel class."

"Good luck. Do you think one of the other students is the murderer?"

"I don't know, but I at least want to see who's there."

"Anybody in particular?"

"For one, I'm curious about an older man named Smith who took an interest in the dead girl."

\*\*\*\*\*

Before talking to the university, Devorkian walked back down the path into the endowment lands and approached Crassner. "Have you got to that leather bag yet?"

"Yeah. We won't go through it completely till we get it back to the lab, but I pulled the wallet. Her ID says she's a student named Pamela Wright. Her driver's license gives an address up north in Thompson. No local address."

"That's okay. I'll get it from the university."

"There's also a set of keys."

\*\*\*\*\*

144

The decor of the room was all cherry wood and royal blue carpet. A highly manicured and perfectly stylish young woman sat behind a cherry wood desk typing briskly on a state-of-the-art computer. Devorkian, sitting on a plush chair against a side wall, did not look out of place in his tailored suit. But he did not dominate the scene as he did most scenes.

The phone buzzed discreetly, and the young woman punched a button. She smiled condescendingly toward Devorkian and spoke in a pleasant voice. "Dr. Randolph will see you now."

Devorkian smiled, rose, opened a solid cherry wood door and passed into an even more luxurious office.

Dr. Julian Randolph, academic vice-president for Assiniboine University, looked up, got up out of his chair, and walked around his massive cherry wood desk to greet his visitor. "Good morning, Detective Devorkian."

"Good morning, Dr. Randolph. It is good of you to see me so promptly." Devorkian had been waiting fifteen minutes, during which time Dr. Randolph had apparently had no other visitors.

The greetings accomplished, Dr. Randolph walked back around the cherry wood desk to his high-backed, black leather executive chair. "Now, Detective Devorkian, how can I help you today?"

"Dr. Randolph, I am sorry to have to inform you that another of your students has been murdered. Her body was discovered this morning in the endowment lands."

Dr. Randolph's face had a grave expression. "I assumed something must have happened when there was so much police activity this morning in parking lot D."

But Devorkian noted to himself that Dr. Randolph had not come out to see personally what was going on. He continued. "Although we do not want this information released publicly yet, we believe the student's name was Pamela Wright."

"Pamela Wright?"

"Yes. Do you know her?"

Dr. Randolph had turned slightly pale. "Pamela Wright is one of our most prized students. Her father is Aaron Wright, president and CEO of Churchill River Mining and Exploration and one of the largest donors to Assiniboine University. This is very serious."

"Dr. Randolph, it was very serious when Lorraine Malthus was killed."

"If you had done your job properly when Ms. Malthus was killed," Randolph said evenly, "this would not have happened."

\*\*\*\*\*

"So what happened?" Hosschuk asked. Did you get the list of students?"

"I felt like punching that pretentious prig in the face." Devorkian smiled. "But I didn't. I used his self-serving attitude to our advantage. I told him if he didn't give me the list, I would tell her father, a Mr. Aaron Wright, that the university wasn't helping us to find Pamela's killer."

"What'd he say to that?"

"He hemmed and hawed and talked about student privacy and human rights and university policy—but in the end he gave me the list."

"This Aaron Wright must be an important guy."

"He's one of the biggest financial contributors to the university."

"Oh. So, anyone interesting on the list?"

Devorkian smiled and handed over a sheet of paper. It contained twenty-three names:

Auxier, Colin
Baerg, Richard
Bal, Rami
Borden, Elizabeth
Chan, Mabel
Chu, Rachel
Friesen, Peter
Gill, Ranjit
Hamilton, Don
Hopkins, Stanley
Horcoff, David
Mann, Brendan
Pembroke, Molly
Richard, Pierre
Singh, Balbinder
Smyth, John
Stankowski, David
Tapinski, Tyler

Uluchuk, Derek
Unger, Bradley
Wall, Elijah
Walker, William
Wright, Pamela

Hosschuk studied the list.

"Anything strike you?" Devorkian asked.

"It's not a very big class."

"It's an extra evening class, offered for those students who couldn't get into it in the regular timeslot."

"Pamela Wright and Molly Pembroke are on the list. And that Don Hamilton Molly mentioned. And the old guy, Mr. Smyth...Hey, remember a while ago when I brought up that old case a few years ago when that religious writer saw a murder from an airplane? Wasn't his name John Smyth?"

Devorkian rolled his eyes. "Yes, John Smyth, but there's no way this could be the same man."

"Why not? This one's got the same unusual spelling of Smyth, with a Y."

"Believe me, it can't be the same man. I told you before there's no way that man would be anywhere near a university campus. He's not intellectual enough."

"But he helped solve that other case."

"He happened to be in the right place at the right time. He was lucky, not intelligent."

"Are you sure?"

"Yes, I'm sure. I'll prove it once we've got the contact information."

Hosschuk stared at the list. "You just got the names and student ID numbers? You don't have contact information?"

"Randolph gave me the list but said it would take some time to pull all the other data out of the computer." Devorkian shook his head. "Look at the list again. You're missing something obvious."

Hosschuk was silent a moment. "Meghan's boyfriend."

"Right. David Horcoff."

"We going to pick him up?"

"Not yet. I want to see what's on the surveillance tapes first. Did you get the tapes from the supermarket?"

"Yes. There are three that show some of the parking lot and the edge of the endowment lands, but I think we'll get most of the information from one of them. It shows the path entrance. The other two are on the sides of the building, but they're pointed toward the sides of the parking lot and just show a bit of the endowment lands in the background. I've taken them all down to the lab."

"Get any other ones?"

"Nothing from the businesses on the other side of the supermarket. They're focused on their own buildings, and the supermarket's between them and the endowment lands."

"What about along University Avenue?"

"There's mostly houses on the other side of the street. A couple had security cameras, but the quality and the angles aren't great. They certainly don't cover all of that side of the endowment lands. But there is a fence and no path entrances on that side."

"To keep out the non-university riffraff." Devorkian shrugged. "The fence is what, six-foot chainlink? It's still climbable. It depends on whether she was killed in the endowment lands. It would be a bit awkward trying to throw a body over that fence. And in that case, the body would probably still be there, not in the middle of the endowment lands near the central path."

"But if she was killed in the woods, the killer could have got in that way."

"It's possible. If so, all our camera work will be a waste of time."

"What about the other side?"

"Along the river? I suppose the killer could have reached the endowment lands by boat. Pretty tricky. With the spring run-off, the water's a few meters above normal, and there are still chunks of ice floating down. Anyway, it's still possible. Later, I want you to go across the river and see if you can find any security cameras facing the river."

"Bit of a long shot, isn't it—to pick up a boat in the background on a dark stretch of river?"

"Yes, a long shot, but we're going to try everything. The lab won't have had time to analyze the other tapes for a few hours anyway, and the autopsy results probably won't be in until tomorrow. But we've got one stop to make before you do that."

"Where?"

"Pamela's condo. Dr. Randolph at least gave me that address."

\*\*\*\*\*

"Mr. Smyth, it's Molly Pembroke."

"Hi, Molly." John Smyth was not surprised Molly had found him at work. Everybody in Grace Evangelical Church knew how to find the editor of *Grace* magazine. "What can I do for you?"

"Mr. Smyth, she's dead."

"Who's dead?"

"Pamela Wright. I found her body this morning when I was walking back to campus through the endowment lands. I thought you should know."

"Dead? What happened to her?"

"I don't know. The police think she was murdered…"

Thought of the springtime murderer popped into Smyth's mind, but he did not mention that to Molly. "That must have been awful for you. I'm so sorry. Are you alright? Did you have someone to talk to?"

"Yes. I already called my mother. I was going to stay here and study, but I think I'll go home on the weekend."

"Good idea."

"Mr. Smyth?"

"Yes."

"I'm glad you told me to talk to her."

"I'm glad too, Molly. At least, you can feel good about that. I think Pamela needed a friend."

Molly's voice caught. "Goodbye, Mr. Smyth."

After he hung up the phone, Smyth sat and pondered for several minutes, while his editorial deadlines pressed ever closer.

\*\*\*\*\*

"The Reinboldt Building?"

The gray limestone stretched thirty stories into the sky, with rows of elaborately carved gargoyles and statues accentuating every balcony and corner.

"Yes," Devorkian answered. "Apparently Pamela needed somewhere to stay while she attended university, so her father bought her a condo in the Reinboldt Building."

"But condos in this building are a few hundred thousand!"

"He can afford it. He probably saw it as an investment, something he could sell in four years for a profit. Now let's see if the keys from Pamela's bag fit the door."

Devorkian, Hosschuk, and three forensics techs rode up the elevator in silence to the twenty-third floor. The door to her condo opened into a living room thirty-five feet long and twenty feet wide, elegantly furnished with floor-to-ceiling windows at the far end offering a spectacular view of the city. From this height, on the flat prairie, it was just possible to discern the curve of the earth on the horizon.

"Better accommodations than the dorm, I presume," Hosschuk said sardonically.

"A little," Devorkian agreed.

To the right were a fully equipped kitchen and a dining room, also with a view of the city. To the left were three doors. The first led to a bedroom with a single bed but with a large desk; it was clearly set up as an office. The middle door led to a bathroom. The third door led to the master bedroom, again elegantly furnished and with a view. On a long dresser were a large assortment of bottles and jars of make-up and perfume. There were also three mannequin heads, two of them adorned with blonde wigs.

"Does she live here alone?" Hosschuk asked.

"Apparently. There are no clothes or personal effects in the other bedroom," Devorkian answered. He paused. "What's missing?"

Hosschuk pondered. "A third wig?"

"Perhaps. What's missing is a computer. There's no computer in the office, and there was no laptop in Pamela's bag. Where are her records?"

"Good question."

"Why don't you go look for surveillance cameras on the other side of the river, and I'll see if I can find a diary or an address book or anything like that here."

# Chapter 34

*Friday, April 9*

Hosschuk wiped at his bleary eyes and sipped his coffee. Across the desk, Devorkian's black suit was lint-free. His white shirt gleamed in the early morning sun streaming through the window.

"How did you make out finding surveillance cameras across the river?" Devorkian asked.

Hosschuk shrugged. "You would think," he said, "with the legislative buildings over there and all the bank towers, that somebody would have a camera trained on the river."

"So if terrorists ever stage an attack on the legislative buildings, they'd be wise to come down the river?"

"Around here, ticked-off taxpayers are more likely than terrorists, if you ask me." Hosschuk shrugged again. "I finally found a couple of cameras that showed some of the river from bad angles."

"Is there anything on the tapes?"

"Grainy black-and-wide video of a black river in the shadow of the woods at midnight, taken from a kilometer away? Technicians said they'd work on it, but they didn't sound very hopeful."

"Well, if the cameras even picked up movement on the river, it would be worth something. They're still working on the video from this side of the river anyway."

"Did they find anything there?" Hosschuk asked.

"They said it would take days to analyze it all, but they'd have some ready to show us in half an hour."

"What did you find in Pamela's condo?"

"Not much. A lot of clothes and personal items, but nothing that would give us any hint who her killer was. We have not found a computer or a cell phone."

"Maybe the motive was robbery in this case."

"I doubt it. Her shoes are also missing."

Hosschuk pondered that. "What about the autopsy?"

"Abner Lazarenko dropped his report off an hour ago."

"What's it say?"

Devorkian picked up a file from the desk. "As he told us before, from body temperature, time of death is estimated about midnight, give or take an hour or two either way. She was strangled. That would have required considerable strength, but she was not a big woman, so that does not tell us much. She had eaten some hours before death, and there was no alcohol in her system. She was not a virgin—"

"I could have guessed that from the red miniskirt and the black lace panties." Hosschuk interrupted.

Devorkian scowled and continued. "She was not a virgin, but there was no evidence of recent sexual activity."

"So no DNA?"

"Not that way. They also scraped her fingernails, but got only fibers, no skin cells."

"So, she may have fought back, but he was wearing gloves and a coat?"

"That's certainly one possibility."

"Any sign of other trauma?"

"Some incidental bruises, but they may have been there before the attack. And lividity suggests she was killed somewhere else and moved."

Hosschuk thought for a moment. "The details are alright. Sounds like the same man."

"It certainly does," Devorkian agreed.

"But we are no nearer figuring out who he is."

"Maybe not. Maybe the trace fibers on the body will tell us something, and we do have the videotapes."

"Maybe."

"But there may be a way to get a DNA match."

"How?"

"She was pregnant."

"Do you think that might be why she was killed, that the killer was the one who got her pregnant?"

"Maybe, but the killer might not have known she was pregnant. She was only about a month along. And remember, since none of the victims was sexually assaulted, we think he might be impotent."

Hosschuk pondered that a moment. "Anything else?"

"Yes. She had had breast implant surgery, and she was wearing a blonde wig."

"The missing wig," Hosschuk said, "What color was her own hair?"

"A somewhat darker shade of blonde." He smiled. "Someone had spent a lot of money to enhance her appearance."

"Who?"

"My guess is she did—using Daddy's money, of course."

*****

Mike Madrigal was a paunchy thirty-something in an oversized T-shirt with untidy curly black hair. He was sitting in front of a computer keyboard with six monitors in two banks.

"The three cameras from parking lot D are in the top row, and the three cameras from the supermarket on the east side of the woods are on the bottom. I have coordinated them chronologically." He didn't look up from the monitors, apparently finding digital humans more interesting than live ones.

"What about the other cameras?" Hosschuk asked.

"Haven't got to them yet," Madrigal answered. "I'll integrate them later if there's anything worthwhile on them. This stuff takes time."

Hosschuk held up his hands. "No problem."

"Parking lot D is a very busy place," Madrigal continued. "Evening classes apparently finish shortly before ten, because about ten o'clock there is big rush of people coming to their cars and driving away for about twenty minutes. Then it slows down, and by ten-thirty the lot is pretty well empty."

"In that rush of people, did anybody go into the endowment lands?" Devorkian asked.

"I didn't see anyone when I went through the tapes, but I'll go through them again frame by frame later and let you know. But there were some people who walked through the parking lot and went onto University Avenue."

"Get images of those people if you can, later on," Devorkian said.

"Okay, there's maybe a few dozen people, and we'll only get back shots of a lot of them."

"Do your best."

"Right."

"What about the tapes from the supermarket parking lot?"

"Same thing. It looks like the store shut down about eleven, but there weren't many people there after about nine-thirty. After that, everybody parked near the store, and pretty well nobody went near the woods."

"Endowment lands," Devorkian corrected.

Madrigal shrugged. "Now, I've set the tapes to start at ten forty-five." He pointed toward a digital read-out on the bottom of one of the monitors.

Devorkian and Hosschuk stared at the screens. The parking lots were deserted, except for a few cars in parking lot D. A dark figure appeared in one of the screens of the top row.

"Who's that?" Hosschuk asked.

"Don't know," Madrigal said. "We can probably enhance the license plates on the cars and pick up the plate number. I'll do that later. See, he goes over to the Lexus, gets in, and then here's the funny thing. He just sits there in the car for the next twenty minutes."

"I would have chosen the Lexus over that old station wagon too," Hosschuk said. "But what's he doing, talking on a cell phone?"

"The camera on the left has a better angle, but it's farther away. When I first saw it, I zoomed in a bit to try to figure out what he was doing. I'll work on it more later. As near as I can tell, he just sits there staring straight ahead."

"At the endowment lands," Devorkian said.

"I guess so." Madrigal shrugged.

The images on the screen became blurry as Madrigal speeded up the images. "Nothing happens for twenty minutes," he said, "until these three guys show up."

Three figures appeared in the screens from the direction of University Avenue and cut across parking lot D on an angle. One was taller and broader than the other two. One of the shorter men was thinner than the other and had a thin face with a discernibly sharper nose and long hair.

"Bunch of students?" Hosschuk asked. "They walk like they're young."

"Could be," Madrigal answered. "They just keep walking across the parking lot and onto campus."

As they disappeared from view, another figure appeared on screen from the direction of University Avenue. This one was much shorter. He was carrying a briefcase in one hand and a box in the other. As he entered the lot, he looked up at the center camera.

"See!" Hosschuk exclaimed. "I told you. Short guy with a beard. It's that Smyth guy, the religious writer."

"It can't be," Devorkian breathed.

"But look, he's going over to that beat-up old station wagon. That looks just like the one he used to drive."

"You'd have thought he would have bought a new one by now," Devorkian said.

"Here's something else interesting," Madrigal said. "The two cars are parked just a few stalls away from each other. As soon as this new guy gets close to them, the other guy suddenly starts his car and peels out of there."

They could see the Lexus indeed back up suddenly, turn and drive quickly out of the parking lot toward University Avenue.

"It's like he didn't want anybody seeing him doing whatever it was he was doing," Hosschuk suggested.

"Maybe," Devorkian said.

"Okay," Madrigal continued. "New guy gets into the old station wagon, and he leaves too. Then it gets quiet again." The screens became blurry as Madrigal fast forwarded. "Nothing happens till about midnight and then it gets busy, like rush hour." After a few moments, the screens stabilized again. "At ten minutes to twelve, this guy walks into the woods from the supermarket parking lot."

Hosschuk and Devorkian stared closely at the screen. The figure walking across the screen appeared to be a young male. He was dressed in a long dark coat and had very dark hair. He walked with a slouch, head down.

"Does he remind you of anyone?" Devorkian asked.

"He looks familiar," Hosschuk answered, "but I can't quite place him."

"I'll try to get you a close-up later," Madrigal said. "Now, just two minutes later, at eleven fifty-two, on the other side, this guy comes from somewhere on campus, crosses parking lot D, and goes into the woods."

This man was tall. He moved quickly and kept looking behind him.

"He looks nervous," Hosschuk suggested. "And he looks like the tallest of the first three guys who walked across the parking lot to the campus."

"Close," Madrigal said. "I wondered too. So I went back and checked. There are slight differences in the clothes."

The screen turned blurry for a few seconds. "Then, at eleven fifty-nine, this guy comes down the sidewalk from that building…"

"The Riel Building," Devorkian said.

"Okay," Madrigal continued. "He comes down the sidewalk, walks across the parking lot on an angle and goes into the woods down there on the path by the river."

The man in question was of average height and slightly overweight.

"Is that a uniform?" Hosschuk asked. "His pants and shirt match."

The man had a jacket on, but it was unzipped.

"I think he might be a janitor," Madrigal suggested. "And it looks like he pulls something out of his pocket just before he goes into the woods."

"A weapon?" Hosschuk asked.

"From the close-up, I would guess a pack of cigarettes," Madrigal answered, "but I'll enhance that image too and find out for sure."

This time the screen did not get blurry.

Madrigal continued, "Just two minutes after that…"

"That's her!" Hosschuk blurted out.

A blonde woman in a long leather coat, her head down, was walking quickly across the parking lot headed for the endowment lands, but she entered the central path, not the path down by the river.

"She came from the same building," Hosschuk said.

"Looks like it," Madrigal agreed.

The screen became blurry again. "Now, at twelve-o-nine, this guy walks across the same way."

This man was dressed in a well-tailored black leather overcoat and had dark bushy hair.

"What are they doing, having a convention?" Hosschuk questioned.

"The endowment lands comprise over a hundred acres," Devorkian said. There are several different paths. They might not even have seen each other."

"Well, somebody ran into Pamela Wright," Hosschuk countered.

"Wait a minute," Devorkian said, pointing at the screen. "Is he holding something in his arm?"

Madrigal backed the video up a few frames. "Looks like it, but I'm not sure what. I'll enhance it later."

"Okay," Devorkian said.

The video started playing forward again. "We're not done yet," Madrigal said. "At twelve twenty-three, this guy walks out the other side."

"He doesn't look like any of the people we saw walk in," Hosschuk said.

"He isn't," Madrigal said. "I think he's a homeless guy, probably sleeps in the woods and is just getting up to see what he can find to scrounge at night."

"You mean he went in much earlier?" Devorkian asked.

"Sure." Madrigal shrugged.

"Have you seen when he went in?"

"No," Madrigal answered. "That might take a while to find. If he went in while it was still light, there were hundreds of people going in and out then, and we'll have to check them all."

The homeless man shuffled. He wore an old baseball cap, a tattered army fatigue jacket, and what looked like blue jeans. He passed out of sight around the corner of the supermarket.

"At about the same time, twelve twenty-four," Madrigal continued, "the guy that looks like a janitor comes out of the woods down by the river and goes back across the parking lot to the building."

The screen became blurry again, then clear. Madrigal said, "At twelve thirty-one, this guy comes back out." It was the older man in the well-tailored overcoat. He came out of the woods onto parking lot D, not by the central path but by another near University Avenue. He headed toward the campus and passed out of range of the cameras.

"Now, this is interesting," Madrigal continued. "At twelve thirty-three, the homeless guy goes back into the woods with a shopping cart full of garbage bags." The man in the camouflage army jacket could be seen pushing a cart into the endowment lands along the central path from the supermarket parking lot.

"Interesting," Devorkian said.

"It's his stuff." Hosschuk shrugged.

"But if he sleeps in the endowment lands, where did he leave his stuff?" Devorkian asked.

"Nobody is going to steal it."

"But somebody might throw it out."

Madrigal interrupted the exchange. "Now, at twelve-thirty five, this guy comes out onto parking lot D." It was the taller, younger, nervous-looking man. He came out by the same path as the well-dressed man, but, instead of heading toward campus, he turned down University Avenue.

The picture became blurry and clear again. "At twelve forty-seven, the homeless guy comes out again," Madrigal said. The man in the camouflage army jacket could be seen coming back out of the endowment lands onto the supermarket parking lot by the same central path as he had used to go in. He was pushing the same shopping cart loaded with garbage bags.

More blurred images. "Finally," Madrigal said, "at one-o-four, this man comes out." It was the young male with the very dark hair and the long dark coat, coming out onto parking lot D by the path close to the river. He was still slouching but was shaking visibly.

"He looks scared," Hosschuk said, "like he has just committed a murder."

"He was in there the whole time," Devorkian mused.

"And that's it," Madrigal concluded. "There's nothing more till the next morning. Everybody is out."

"Except for Pamela Wright," Devorkian said.

"We know she went in at twelve-o-one and never came out," Hosschuk said. "Since everyone else was out by one-o-four, that means she must have been dead by then."

"That's consistent with what the coroner said," Devorkian observed.

Hosschuk nodded. "And that also means that one of those people we saw go into the woods must have killed her."

"Unless someone else sneaked in some other way," Devorkian cautioned.

There was a prolonged silence as the men pondered what they had seen.

"What's next?" Hosschuk asked finally.

"We try to identify every one of those people," Devorkian said. He turned to Madrigal. "Can you get me an edited CD just showing all of the people going in and out?"

"Sure."

"And now," Devorkian said, nodding to Hosschuk, "it's time to go and see the one person we can identify."

"John Smyth?" Hosschuk said. "I told you we should be talking to him even before we saw him on the tape."

Devorkian stared hard at Hosschuk. "We aren't going to talk to John Smyth. I am. You see if you can find that homeless man."

*****

Beautiful, blonde-haired Rachel looked up from her computer.

Devorkian had never been to John Smyth's office. Whatever he had expected, he had not expected this. The low-ceilinged, older, two-story brick building on an inner-city street fit what he knew of John Smyth. But Rachel was something else. He had pictured a frumpy, middle-aged secretary perhaps, but certainly not Rachel.

He smiled. "I'd like to see John Smyth."

Rachel smiled back. Her smile radiated sunshine. "Your name, please?"

"Detective Devorkian from the Winnipeg Police Department."

The smile wavered only slightly. "Come this way."

Rachel led the way down a very short hall to a small, cluttered office. "John, there's a Detective Devorkian here to see you."

Devorkian went in, shut the door behind him and sat in one of the two chairs in front of Smyth's desk. Smyth stood, then settled back down into his chair when Devorkian did not offer to shake hands.

"That's quite the secretary you have," Devorkian observed.

"She's very…efficient," Smyth answered. "Good morning, Detective. It's been quite a while since I last saw you."

Devorkian studied Smyth a moment, then looked around the room. Papers and magazines seemed to be stacked everywhere.

"I presume you are here about Pamela Wright?" Smyth asked.

Devorkian quickly refocused his eyes on Smyth. "What do you know about Pamela Wright?"

"I understand that she's dead, that she was found yesterday morning in the endowment lands."

"How do you know that?" Devorkian snapped. "We haven't released her name to the public."

"Molly Pembroke phoned me yesterday."

"Oh."

"I presume you are here because I was on the surveillance tape."

"What surveillance tape?" Devorkian had been deliberately quiet in order to let Smyth talk, but he realized he was losing control of the direction of the interview.

"The tape from the surveillance cameras you had installed in parking lot D."

"How do you know about them?"

"Tyler Tapinski told us about them."

"Who's he?"

"He's a student. He said he was on the university committee that approved installing the cameras."

"Who's 'us'? Who did he tell?"

"A group of students from the evening class I've been taking."

"Did he tell anyone else?"

"I don't know," Smyth said, "but Tyler said he doesn't believe in secrets, so I wouldn't be surprised if he told other people."

Devorkian sighed. "I think you had better come down to the station. There is some video I'd like you to look at." He paused. "We'll go in my car."

*****

"So you finally arrested him?" Hosschuk smiled.

Devorkian did not. "Mr. Smyth is here voluntarily. He is going to take a look at the video tapes and see if he recognizes anyone."

Devorkian led Smyth and Hosschuk into a small room with a television. When he had inserted the tape, he said, "Now, Mr. Smyth, the video quality is not great. There are a lot of people on the university campus, and you may not recognize anyone, so don't suggest you know someone if you're not sure."

Smyth leaned forward as the tape began to play. "I think that's Don Henderson," he said almost immediately. "He's an English professor and has an office in the Riel Building next to the parking lot."

Hosschuk wrote the name down on a pad.

The tape moved forward until three students appeared crossing the parking lot to the university. "That's probably Tyler Tapinski, Derek Uluchuk, and Brendan Mann," Smyth said. "They're in my study group, and we were just coming back to campus."

"Is that the same study group Molly Pembroke is in?" Devorkian asked.

"Yes. We meet after class every week at The Mystery of Chocolate."

At that point, Smyth himself appeared in the frame and peered up at the camera.

"Apparently one of the students, Mr. Tapinski, told the other students about the cameras," Devorkian said drily. Hosschuk was busily writing down names and didn't look up.

The video was now showing the figure in black approaching the endowment lands from the supermarket side. Smyth drew in his breath sharply.

"Recognize him?" Devorkian asked.

"I think it might be David Horcoff," Smyth said. "He's part of the study group, too, but he stayed behind at The Mystery of Chocolate after we left."

Devorkian nodded.

The video showed a tall, well-built student approaching the endowment lands across parking lot D. "That might be Don Hamilton," Smyth said. "He wears a university jacket like that."

Hosschuk wrote that name down too.

"I don't know him," Smyth said when the next figure walked across the parking lot. He paused. "But it might be the janitor from the Riel Building."

When the next figure appeared, Smyth caught his breath.

"That's Pamela Wright, of course," Devorkian said.

Smyth didn't say anything for a moment. "But why would she walk into the endowment lands alone at night?"

"Good question," Devorkian answered. "We think she might have been meeting someone. Do you know who it might have been?"

Smyth shook his head.

"Molly Pembroke said Pamela might have been dating Don Hamilton," Devorkian pressed. "Do you think she might have been meeting him?"

Smyth considered. "It's possible. There was a rumor that she was dating him, and she told Molly she couldn't come to the study group because she had dates after class. But I don't know anything about all of that."

A man with black, bushy hair and wearing a well-tailored, black leather overcoat had come into the camera frame.

"Do you have any idea who that is?" Devorkian asked.

"I'm not sure," Smyth answered. "It might be Dr. Kingston. I saw him once wearing a coat like that. He teaches Greek or Latin or something like that."

The next image on the screen was wearing blue jeans, a tattered army fatigue jacket and an old baseball cap and walked across the parking lot on the other side of the endowment lands heading toward the supermarket.

"I have no idea who that is," Smyth said.

"Are you sure?" Hosschuk asked. "You knew everybody else."

"Pretty sure," Smyth said. "There is something vaguely familiar about him, but I don't know him. Maybe he just looks like somebody I know, or maybe he is just someone I saw once on the street."

Smyth watched the rest of the tape, but could offer nothing new. The second appearance of the people on the tapes merely confirmed the identifications he had already given.

"Thank you, Mr. Smyth," Devorkian said. "Is there anything else you can tell me about any of these people?"

"Not that I can think of."

"If you think of anything, let me know," Devorkian said with a smile. "I'll have an officer drive you back to work."

*****

"I told you that Smyth would know something useful. He identified almost everyone on the tape." Hosschuk was breaking the cardinal rule

162

that an underling should never remind his superior that he had been right and the superior had been wrong.

"That's only because they were all in the same class with him and the victim," Devorkian protested. "He just happened to be in the right place at the right time."

"He has a habit of doing that," Hosschuk replied, digging the hole deeper.

"Speaking of being where you're supposed to be, what have you found out?" Deovorkian asked.

"Smyth is right about Don Henderson. Mike blew up the image of the license plate, and it was Henderson's car," Hosschuk answered. "He got a blow-up of Smyth's license plate, too, but we already knew whose car that was."

"What about the homeless man?"

"Nothing yet, but I've called in Constable Martin, one of the downtown beat cops, to see if he can help us. He should be here soon."

*****

"Constable Martin, we would like you to look at this tape and see if you recognize the man in it."

Constable Gordon Martin, a tall, barrel-chested man, overflowed the chair placed in front of the television set. He sat passively while the grainy image of a man in an old baseball cap, a tattered army fatigue jacket, and blue jeans ambled across the screen, first alone and then pushing a shopping cart.

"Well?" Devorkian asked.

"The face is not visible," Martin replied calmly, "but it looks like Sergeant Pepper."

"From the Lonely Hearts Club Band?" Devorkian asked drily. "Maybe we'll run some more tape and see if you recognize Paul McCartney."

Martin seemed not to notice the sarcasm. "Sergeant Pepper is the name we have for this homeless guy who wanders around the downtown core. Always wears an army camouflage jacket."

"What's his real name?" Devorkian asked.

"Don't know. I don't think we've ever actually arrested him."

"Is he an army vet?"

"I don't know that either," Martin said. "He seems to be a veteran of some war, but maybe only the war on drugs."

Devorkian raised a quizzical eyebrow.

Martin explained, "His brain is fried. It might be post-traumatic shock from a war or maybe it's from meth or some other drug. He doesn't make any sense when we try to talk to him. That's why we call him Sergeant Pepper, because of the jacket and because he reminds us of a drug-happy hippie."

"Does he push around a shopping cart?"

"Sure. Most of them do."

"What's in it?"

"Don't know. I never searched it. Probably clothes and empties."

"Where does he live?"

"Can't really call it living. He's a regular in the downtown area. I think he sleeps outside or in one of the shelters."

"Have you ever seen him outside of the downtown area, near the university?" Devorkian asked.

"Nope," Martin answered, "but I never go near the university either."

"What would he be doing in the endowment lands?"

"Don't know. Could be looking for empties."

"Could he sleep there?"

"Sometimes maybe."

"Can you tell me anything else about him?"

"Nope. Don't know much myself. He's only been around for two or three years, don't know where he came from. You could always ask Harry Collins over at Grace Mission. He might know something."

"Do you think Sergeant Pepper is capable of murder?"

"Capable is not a word we use for Pepper," Martin answered. "As I said, he doesn't make any sense. I have no idea what goes on inside his head or what he might do."

"Do you think you could find him and bring him in?"

"Shouldn't be too hard."

"We'll send you out with a paddy wagon. Bring in his shopping cart too."

"Make a nice change from walking."

"And this Harry Collins—where would I find him?"

"At Grace Mission on north Main Street. Do you want me to ask him to come in? He doesn't like cops coming to the mission. He says it drives away his customers."

Devorkian nodded. "That would be helpful."

*****

"What do you think?" Devorkian asked when Martin had gone.

"About what, Martin or Sergeant Pepper?" Hosschuk answered.

Devorkian smiled. "Martin is one of those beat cops who is so competent that he'll never get promoted. He's too valuable."

Hosschuk grinned back. "But what he said about Sergeant Pepper turning up is interesting."

"Precisely," Devorkian answered grimly. "He showed up in Winnipeg about the time the murders started." Devorkian was silent for several minutes, then spoke again. "It's a classic English country manor murder mystery."

"What?"

"It's a classic English country manor murder mystery."

Seeing the confused look on Hosschuk's face, Devorkian sighed and explained. "It's a type of murder mystery novel. A murder is committed in an isolated English country manor—or on a boat or on an airplane or on a train—so there are a limited number of suspects, and the reader knows one of them must have done it."

Hosschuk asked, "When you were at university, did you take that Mystery Novel course that Smyth and Pamela Wright were in?"

Devorkian shook his head. "No. It wasn't offered then. But I could probably teach it."

Hosschuk grinned. "I know! The butler did it!"

Devorkian smiled back. "Yes, in the books, it's usually the least likely suspect, the servant, the man standing quietly in the background who did it. It doesn't usually turn out to be that way in real life. In real life, it is usually the most obvious suspect." Devorkian's face turned serious. "Besides, in this case, we don't have a butler."

"But we have a janitor." Hosschuk thought a moment. "So, in this case, who is the most obvious suspect?"

"Obviously the one who was already a suspect in one of the other murders."

"David Horcoff."

Devorkian nodded.

"So, do we arrest Horcoff?"

"No," Devorkian said. "We do not jump to conclusions. We have a limited number of suspects. We know Pamela Wright must have been murdered by one of the men who went into the endowment lands that night. So, we interview and investigate every one of them and figure out which one of them did it." He paused and smiled. "But we will make sure we handle David Horcoff very carefully, by the book. I don't want any mistakes."

*****

"Thank you for coming in, Mr. Collins," Devorkian said smoothly.

Harry Collins was the short, fat, bald-headed director of Grace Mission in Winnipeg's depressing inner city. "That's okay," he answered. "I'd rather do it this way. Last year, a policeman came in to ask me a question, and half of our clients wouldn't come near the mission for a month."

Devorkian smiled. "That won't happen this time."

"Constable Martin said you wanted to ask me about Sergeant Pepper?"

"Yes," Devorkian answered. "Why do you call him that?"

"At the Mission, we call people by their street names. It is one way of affirming their dignity. If they want to be called Pinocchio, we call them Pinocchio."

"And this man has asked to be called Sergeant Pepper?"

"In his case, it is what everybody calls him. He answers to it, so that's what we call him." Collins explained further, "It may not be what he wants to be called, but it is better than being called by his real name. Many people on the street don't want to reveal their true identities, they don't want to risk being found in their current condition by anybody they might have known in their old lives."

"Do you have any idea what Sergeant Pepper's real name might be?"

"I think it's Bob."

"Bob?" For once, Devorkian was almost speechless.

"Sorry," Collins elaborated. "I don't know his last name."

"What else can you tell me about Bob?"

"He's been coming to Grace Mission for a little over two years, showed up out of the blue one spring. He comes for meals three or four days a week. We give him clothes sometimes."

"Where does he sleep? Does he have a place to stay?"

"In the winter, he sleeps on a mat on our floor. We have a shelter program with some funding from the city. The rest of the year, I have no idea."

"Where has he been sleeping this week? At the mission?"

Collins reflected for a moment. "No," he said. "When the weather turned a little warmer a few days ago, he stopped coming in. I haven't seen him for about a week."

"Do you know where he comes from? Was he ever in the military? Does he have an accent?"

"I don't know where he's from, I have no idea about whether he might have been in the military, and it's rather hard to place his accent. He slurs. That's about it."

Devorkian was incredulous. "He's been coming to your mission for two years and that's all you know? Don't you talk to him?"

"Oh, we talk to him. He just doesn't talk back much. We do our best, but you can't push street people to open up. Otherwise, they would stop coming. Many of them have deep-seated problems with trust. We just have to be patient and wait for them to talk to us. Sometimes it takes years to develop trust."

"Well, when you do talk to Bob, what do you talk about?"

Collins reflected. "Bob's a bit different," he said finally. "You can't really have a conversation with him. We say something. If he's in the right mood, he might say something back, but it doesn't necessarily have any relationship to what we said."

"If his mind is that far gone, how does he survive?"

Collins reflected. "People on the street just seem to know how to find food and shelter and other things they need, almost by instinct."

"Is he capable of murder?"

The question caught Collins off guard, as it was designed to do. He reflected a moment and then said, "We are all capable of murder. I don't know if he has the capacity to commit premeditated murder."

"Is he prone to violent outbursts?"

Collins reflected again. "No, I would say almost the opposite. He is slow and methodical."

"Have you ever known him to commit a crime?"

"No."

"Is he an alcoholic or a drug addict?"

"You know," Collins said thoughtfully, "I don't think he is. I wouldn't be surprised to learn that he used to use drugs—that might explain his current mental state—but I don't think he is currently drinking or using drugs. He is the same all the time, no highs or lows. That is unusual for our clientele."

"Could he be faking?"

"They're all faking, Detective," Collins said. "They all hide things. They all have delusions. They lie. But if you're suggesting that he is perfectly normal and just pretending to be out of it, I don't think so. What would be the point?"

*****

"What do you think?" Devorkian asked Hosschuk when Collins was gone.

"I don't know," Hosschuk answered. "Pepper sounds crazy enough to commit murder. But he may be too crazy to have committed these murders. If he doesn't know what day it is, how could he plan to kill every April?"

"That's where you're wrong," Devorkian said. "The timing fits perfectly. He arrived in Winnipeg two years ago, just before the first murder. And he doesn't plan to kill every April. He doesn't plan anything. The dates aren't that precise. When spring comes, he moves outdoors, and that's when the killing happens. That may be the trigger, springtime in Winnipeg."

*****

Friday afternoon is the end of the work week for many people, but not for policemen in the middle of a homicide investigation.

The janitor was pushing his industrial-strength vacuum down the hallway of the second floor of the Riel Building when it stopped abruptly. Two men were standing in front of him. The taller man in the immaculate suit had his foot planted firmly on the vacuum head. He flashed his badge in front of the startled face of the janitor. It took him a few seconds to react, by turning off the vacuum.

The tall man smiled. "My name is Detective Devorkian. Is there somewhere we can talk?"

The janitor pointed. "There's a seminar room at the end of the hall." He unplugged the vacuum and began pushing it toward the room. When he reached it, he pulled out a key chain and unlocked the door, pushing the vacuum inside.

"Is that really necessary?" asked the other man, a muscular younger man with blond hair.

"Yeah," the janitor replied. "You'd be surprised what students will steal."

"No, I wouldn't," Devorkian said, smiling again. "Why don't we sit down?"

They sat, with Devorkian and Hosschuk on one side of a long table and the janitor on the other.

"Could you please show us some identification?" Devorkian asked.

The janitor pulled out a plastic university ID card with his picture, a number, the name Michael Brown, and the phrase "custodial staff."

"So, Mr. Brown," Devorkian continued. "Do you regularly work the night shift in this building?"

Brown nodded. "Usually."

"How long have you worked here?"

"At the university? About four years."

"You were working last night?"

"Sure." Brown was a round-faced man of medium height. He appeared to be in his thirties. Up to this point, he had seemed at ease.

"And two nights ago, at eleven-fifty-nine, you walked out of this building, across parking lot D, and into the endowment lands."

Brown's face paled noticeably. He took a breath and patted the bulge in his shirt pocket. "That'd be about right. It's a non-smoking campus. I went outside to have a cigarette," he said, adding, "It was time for my break."

"And you were in the endowment lands twenty-five minutes."

Brown was clearly nervous now. He twitched. "So, I had two cigarettes. My supervisor don't care as long as I get my work done by the end of the shift."

Devorkian paused, his dark eyes boring into Brown. "You went into the endowment lands exactly two minutes before a young woman, a student. Did you see her?"

"No, I didn't see anyone." His eyes widened. "You mean it was the girl who was killed?"

"Precisely, Mr. Brown," Devorkian said. "You were in the woods at precisely the time the young woman was in the same woods being murdered."

Brown said nothing, his mouth open slightly.

"Did you kill her?" Devorkian asked quietly.

"No, of course not."

"Did you see her?"

"No, I just went into the woods a little way down by the river and stood there smoking."

"Did you hear anything?"

Brown reflected. "No, I can't remember hearing anything. It was windy, and the branches were banging against each other a bit."

"Did you see anyone at all, either in the endowment lands or in the parking lot?"

Brown shook his head. "No. I seen no one."

"How about in this building? Did you see anyone here just before you went out for a smoke?"

Brown thought again. "I was on the fourth floor by then. I remember one of the professors was in when I was on the second floor, an older guy."

"Don Henderson?"

"Yeah, I think that's his name. He asked me not to clean his office."

"Was that unusual?"

"No, he does that some nights. He's been working late a lot this month."

"Do you remember the nights last year when the other students were found murdered in the endowment lands?"

Brown shrugged. "I don't remember. I was probably here those nights, but I didn't see anything."

Devorkian smiled. "Thank you, Mr. Brown. You have been helpful."

Brown visibly relaxed.

"Do you like to look at the female students?" Hosschuk asked suddenly.

Brown was caught off guard. "No! Well, sometimes. The pretty ones. But there's not many of them here when I'm working."

Devorkian smiled again.

*****

But even that was not the end of their day. Several hours later, they were back, parking their car in the now vacant parking lot D. They got out and began walking down the central path through the endowment lands. There was light from the parking lot and other lights spaced along the path just close enough together that it was possible to walk without stumbling.

"Pretty murky," Devorkian said, "but you wouldn't need a flashlight if you stayed on this central path."

"Lots of places to hide in wait for someone too," Hosschuk offered.

"But if you were Pamela Wright, would you walk through here at midnight?"

"No. She must have been meeting someone."

"Right. But which one?"

They had come to the place where Pamela Wright's body had been dumped. Devorkian pushed into the bushes. He looked back and pointed at one of the widely spaced lights.

"There's just enough from that light that he could dump the body without needing a flashlight," he said.

"Do you think that's why he chose this spot?" Hosschuk asked.

"Maybe."

They walked on until the path came out into the supermarket parking lot. Devorkian led Hosschuk along the parking lot toward the river and entered the path along the riverbank. After a few steps, he stopped.

"This is a little tougher," Devorkian said.

"Yeah," Hosschuk agreed. "There's a little moonlight, and some light from across the river. You'd probably stumble quite a bit. A flashlight would help. Isn't that a bench up there?"

They walked a little farther to the bench. Hosschuk sat.

"After a while, the eyes adjust," Hosschuk said. "You could probably walk all the way back to the university if you were careful."

They did that and then moved over to the third main path near University Avenue.

"I thought the lights on University Avenue would help more," Hosschuk said. "This is darker than the path by the river."

"I think you're right," Devorkian answered. "And the side paths would probably be worse. But I suppose it depends why you're here. If you're here to commit a murder, you would want it dark."

# Chapter 35

## Saturday, April 10

"Where did you find him?"

"He was wandering on Main Street just north of the city core," Constable Martin answered.

"That would be two or three kilometers from the endowment lands," Devorkian mused.

"About that, but over the bridge."

"What's the point? He could walk over the bridge."

"Sure, but bridges act as barriers, marking territory. The homeless don't usually wander too far from home, so to speak."

"Okay, but Sergeant Pepper may be an exception." Devorkian was staring through the one-way glass at a man in a worn camouflage jacket and a grimy baseball cap of an undetermined color. He had a few days' stubble on his face, and he looked to be somewhere between thirty and fifty. The man was sitting upright in a chair in an interrogation room. A Styrofoam cup of cooling coffee was in front of him.

"Oh, he's exceptional in a lot of ways."

"Did he give you any trouble?"

"He protested, but he didn't fight. He seems pretty passive."

"You brought in his grocery cart?"

"Yes, I took it down to forensics like you said."

Devorkian thought a moment. "Okay, let's see what Sergeant Pepper has to say for himself."

Devorkian entered the room and sat down. He smiled and reached his hand across the table. "Good morning. My name is Detective Devorkian." When the other man said nothing, he added, "What's your name?"

The other man blinked and then responded in a quiet but surprisingly deep voice. "Sergeant Pepper."

Devorkian smiled again. "No, I mean what is your real name?"

The other man immediately snapped a salute. "Sergeant Pepper, sir!"

Devorkian said slowly, "Your name is Bob..."

"Bob doesn't live here anymore," the other responded.

"You sleep and eat at Grace Mission sometimes, don't you?"

"Amazing grace, how sweet the sound that saved a wretch like me," the man recited. His eyes were wide open but shifting constantly around the room.

"But sometimes you sleep in the woods beside the university."

"If you go down in the woods today, you'd better not go alone."

"Why?" Devorkian asked sharply.

"Because every bear that ever there was will gather there for certain because today's the day the teddy bears have their picnic."

Devorkian looked the man over for a few moments. He recognized the old children's song. The man seemed to speak in snatches of quotes from things he had heard. "You like to sleep with teddy bears? Did you ever sleep with this teddy bear?" He pulled a head shot of Pamela Wright out of a file folder and shoved it across the table toward the man.

He glanced at it. "Never saw her before in my life."

"But you strangled her in the woods, didn't you?"

"Never saw her before in my life."

"Did you sleep in the woods near the university two days ago?" Devorkian demanded.

The man blinked and looked around the room. "Don't know where I've been."

"Did you do this to her?" Devorkian slid another photo across the table, this time a close-up of Pamela Wright's body in the woods.

The man looked startled by the photo. "Teddy bears didn't do it. It's sad."

"Did you do it?" Devorkian demanded.

The man shook his head. "How many deaths will it take till he knows that too many people have died?"

"Did you see who did do it?"

"See no evil. Hear no evil. Speak no evil."

"Were you in the woods?"

"Sitting downtown in the railway station, one toke over the line, sweet Jesus."

"How about this woman?" Devorkian slid a head shot of Astrid Andersson across the table.

"Pretty woman."

"Did you kill her too?"

"Pretty woman."

Devorkian jumped to his feet, reached across the table, grabbed the man by the coat lapels and shouted into his face, "Did you kill these women?"

The man blinked and stared back into Devorkian's face. "Pretty woman, just walk on by."

"Did you kill them?" Devorkian said slowly, still holding the man.

"Do no evil," the man replied.

\*\*\*\*\*

"I want fingerprints, DNA, the works," Devorkian said.

"But we haven't charged him," Hosschuk protested. "We have no legal right to take his fingerprints or a DNA sample. It won't stand up in court. The whole case will get thrown out."

"That man isn't going to court," Devorkian growled. He had kept at it for another forty-five minutes, without getting any sensible answers. "That man," he continued, "is homeless and psychologically disturbed. We are merely trying to identify him so we can get him back home where he belongs and get him the help he needs." He turned toward Hosschuk. "Look, if that is an act, it's a very good one. If not, he's too crazy to stand trial. Either way, I want to know if he committed these murders. The evidence may not stand up in a murder trial, but we might be able to have him committed to a psychiatric hospital. If he committed those murders, I don't want him out on the streets. Did forensics find anything?"

Hosschuk was thrown off by the sudden change in direction. "Oh," he said. "There was nothing on his person or in his shopping cart to identify him. He had a wallet, but all it had in it was a few dollars and some change. There was nothing in the cart that links him to the dead women, no souvenirs from the bodies. Forensics have taken some hair and fiber samples for testing, but they didn't find anything obvious."

"Has he been released?" Devorkian asked.

"Yeah," Hosschuk answered. "We took fingerprints and DNA, catalogued all his possessions and then took him back to Main Street. We dropped him off in front of Grace Mission."

"Did he go in?"

"No." Hosschuk smiled. "He walked over to a bus stop bench, unpacked everything out of his cart, emptied all the bags and then repacked everything. I guess he didn't like forensics messing about with his stuff." Hosschuk paused. "Are we done for today?"

"No. We have a visit to make."

*****

The house was not ostentatious, but it was nicely set on a carefully manicured lawn, a well-built structure with a Tudor design and leaded windows.

Devorkian rang the doorbell.

A well-built man with hair graying at the temples answered. He was wearing dress pants, a white shirt, and a sweater.

"Dr. Henderson." Devorkian smiled. "Could we talk with you for a few minutes?"

Henderson paused just slightly. "Certainly, Detective."

He showed them into an immaculately neat living room with expensive couches arranged in front of a massive stone fireplace. He sat down on one while the detectives sat on another, facing him.

"Can I offer you coffee or something else to drink?" Henderson asked.

"No, thank you," Devorkian said. "You said that you knew Meghan Hall. Have you remembered anything else about her or anything from the night she was killed that you can tell us?"

Henderson stared coldly at Devorkian, then said, "No, Detective."

"How about Pamela Wright?"

"What about her?"

"Did you know her?"

"Yes. She was in one of my classes last fall, and before that she was in the Introductory English course where I lectured a couple of times. That course is taught by several of the professors in the department, taking a few lectures each."

"Did you ever talk with her?"

"A couple of times after class, I think, about possible essay topics and that sort of thing."

"Was she ever in your office?"

Henderson paused and frowned. "It's possible. I keep regular office hours, and students do come to talk about assignments and grades and sometimes even to ask questions about books or poems we are studying. But I don't remember Miss Wright ever coming."

"But you remembered her. You don't remember Lorraine Malthus or Astrid Andersson, but you remember Pamela Wright. Why?"

Henderson smiled. "Pamela Wright is a rather memorable individual."

"Why?"

Henderson became serious. "She dressed rather provocatively for one thing, very short skirts in the middle of winter. She drew the attention of a lot of male students, and that meant I had to make sure I kept the students focused on my lecture so she didn't become a distraction. She was also rather flamboyant, always willing to give her opinion in class discussions."

"Were you attracted to her?"

"No, Detective, I was not."

Devorkian remained silent for a few moments. "Did you kill her?"

"No, Detective, I did not."

"Did you see her the night she was killed?"

"No."

"But you were sitting in your car in parking lot D about the time she was killed in the endowment lands. Are you sure you didn't see her?"

"Yes, I am sure I didn't see her." Henderson was starting to sound annoyed.

"What did you see? Did you see anyone else in the endowment lands?"

"No."

"But you sat in your car looking at the endowment lands for quite a while. Why?"

"I was thinking."

"And when some students came along, you immediately drove away."

"Yes."

"Why?"

"I told you, Detective, I was thinking and didn't want to lose my train of thought by talking to anybody."

"Or maybe you didn't want to be seen."

"I didn't care whether I was seen. I just didn't want to talk to anyone just then.

"What were you thinking about?"

Henderson paused, then smiled. "I was thinking about Ulysses."

"Ulysses who?" Hosschuk interjected.

"It's a famous poem by Lord Tennyson. The poem tells the story of Ulysses, who as an old man decided to leave his kingdom in charge of his son Telemachus and to go off to seek a newer world. I was thinking about what that poem could have meant to Tennyson. I think he saw himself as Telemachus, the plodder who was left behind to teach morals to a barbaric nation—note the repetition of the T, E, and S in the two names. I think Tennyson saw Ulysses as his friend Arthur Hallam, the greater man who had died young. Again, note the repetition of the L. In the poem, Ulysses goes west through the straits of Gibraltar, an image of death." He paused and looked at Hosschuk's face. "Well, you asked what I was thinking about."

\*\*\*\*\*

"You're the university guy," Hosschuk said on their way back to their car. "Does that Ulysses thing make any sense to you?"

"Oh, yes. It makes a lot of sense. I think it's an interesting and creative reinterpretation of a famous poem," Devorkian answered. "But I don't believe for a minute that that's what he was thinking about sitting in that car. He may have been thinking about death, but it wasn't Hallam's death. Note the repetition of the N and S in Henderson, and the repetition of the double L in Meghan Hall."

"Do you think he did the killing?" Hosschuk asked.

Devorkian shrugged. "He's hiding something. I just don't know what."

# Chapter 36

### *Sunday, April 12*

"Good morning, John." Don Henderson shook John Smyth's hand in his powerful grip. They were standing in the foyer of Central Grace Evangelical Church after the morning service. "How are you doing?"

"Well, I think I survived Dr. Hemenhof's course." Smyth caught himself. "Sorry. That was the wrong thing to say. You've heard about Pamela Wright?"

"Of course," Henderson answered. "The police came to see me yesterday."

Smyth nodded. "Because you were in the parking lot that night?"

"How did you...? Oh, that's right, you were there too. Did the police talk to you too?"

"Yes, they said what I told them was helpful."

"What did you tell them?"

"Just who some of the people on the surveillance tapes were."

"What surveillance tapes?"

"You didn't know? The police installed surveillance cameras in parking lot D to try to catch whoever's been murdering students each spring."

"No, I didn't know. But I am not in the loop these days. I guess that's how they knew I was there."

"What did you tell them?" Smyth asked.

"Not a lot," Henderson answered. "It is not always wise to tell the police everything."

"Why?"

"Because I think they already see me as a suspect because I knew Meghan Hall."

Smyth nodded.

"Why did you take that course about murder anyway?" Henderson continued. "April is a terrible month. There have been too many deaths." He was looking across the foyer to where the usually bubbly Sheila Hall was standing by herself, staring vacantly into space.

# Chapter 37

## Monday, April 13

"I got it!"

Hosschuk looked up to see Devorkian coming through the doorway. "What did you get?"

"Pamela Wright's transcript."

"Is there anything significant on it?"

"I don't know. I haven't looked at it yet."

Devorkian laid the sheet of paper he was holding on the desk, and the two men began looking it over.

**Pamela Wright #1200129**

| Fall 2012 | Instructor | Grade |
|---|---|---|
| SO100 Introduction to Sociology I | R.R. Smith, B.K. Janzen | 83 |
| EN100 Introductory English I | Faculty | 82 |
| AN100 Introduction to Anthropology I | B.L. Saddat | 81 |
| PY100 Introductory Psychology I | S.K. Magnusson | 85 |
| EC100 Introductory Economics I | H.E. Turner | 75 |

| Spring 2013 | Instructor | Grade |
|---|---|---|
| SO101 Introduction to Sociology II | B.K. Janzen, S.N. Burke | 81 |
| EN101 Introductory English II | Faculty | 80 |
| AN101 Introduction to Anthropology II | B.L. Saddat | 84 |
| PY101 Introductory Psychology II | S.K. Magnusson | 87 |
| EC100 Introductory Economics II | H.E. Turner | 74 |

| Fall 2013 | Instructor | Grade |
|---|---|---|
| PY200 Advanced Psychology I | P.K. Rosenblatt | 86 |
| PY210 Psychological Research Methods I | A.W. Black | 79 |
| PY233 Physiology of the Brain | S.W. Miller | 81 |
| SO200 Advanced Sociology | R.K. Das | 82 |

| EN280 American Literature I | B.L. McGwire | 80 |
|---|---|---|

| Spring 2014 | Instructor | Grade |
|---|---|---|
| PY201 Advanced Psychology II | P.K. Rosenblatt | 88 |
| PY211 Psychological Research Methods II | A.W. Black | 80 |
| PY334 Theories of Personality | A.K. Chang | 89 |
| SO201 Advanced Sociology | R.K. Das | 81 |
| EN281 American Literature II | D.R. Hemenhof | 90 |

| Fall 2014 | Instructor | Grade |
|---|---|---|
| PY335 Introduction to Deviant Psych. | M.W. Pasterski | 85 |
| PY345 Freud, Jung: Historical Psych. I | I.M. Berg | 78 |
| PY361 Psychology of the Child | M.S. Winger | 83 |
| PY315 Issues in American Sociology I | D.S. Maxwell | 89 |
| EN350 The Victorian Novel | D.H. Henderson | 84 |

| Spring 2015 | Instructor | Grade |
|---|---|---|
| PS336 Deviant Psychology II | M.W. Pasterski | Incomplete |
| PY346 Historical Psychology II | I.M. Berg | Incomplete |
| PY362 Adolescent Psychology | M.S. Winger | Incomplete |
| SO316 Issues in American Sociology II | D.S. Maxwell | Incomplete |
| EN341 The Mystery Novel | D.R. Hemenhof | Incomplete |

"What do you think?" Devorkian asked after a bit.

"Her marks are good, but not as good as Meghan Hall's, right?"

"Right."

"And she took a course from Professor Henderson."

"Right." Devorkian began shuffling though some other files and came up with another piece of paper. He laid it beside Pamela Wright's transcript. "Look at that," he said. "She took four courses with David Horcoff, two sociology courses and two English courses."

"That was two years ago," Hosschuk observed.

"Yes, but they are both in the mystery novel course this term."

"Should we pick him up?"

"In due time. I have something else." Devorkian pulled another sheet out of his pocket and laid it on the table. "This is Don Hamilton's transcript."

| Fall 2013 | Instructor | Grade |
|---|---|---|
| SO100 Introduction to Sociology I | R.R. Smith, B.K. Janzen | 74 |
| EN100 Introductory English I | Faculty | 71 |
| PY100 Introductory Psychology I | S.K. Magnusson | 69 |
| KP100 Introduction to Kinesiology I | J.P. Gilliam | 79 |
| BI100 Introduction to Biology I | R.O Hassad | 64 |

| Spring 2014 | Instructor | Grade |
|---|---|---|
| SO101 Introduction to Sociology II | B.K. Janzen, S.N. Burke | 66 |
| EN101 Introductory English II | Faculty | 69 |
| PY101 Introductory Psychology II | S.K. Magnusson | 70 |
| KP101 Introduction to Kinesiology II | J.P. Gilliam | 78 |
| BI101 Introduction to Biology II | R.O Hassad | 65 |

| Fall 2014 | Instructor | Grade |
|---|---|---|
| KP202 Basic Human Anatomy | P.O. Vine | 72 |
| KP214 Contemporary Health Issues | S.M. Kitchener | 71 |
| KP256 Basic Weight Training | P.K. Strang | 81 |
| PY251 Sports Psychology | A.R. Robertson | 69 |
| AN101 Introduction to Anthropology I | B.L. Saddat | 68 |

| Spring 2015 | Instructor | Grade |
|---|---|---|
| KP203 Introduction to Biomechanics | P.O. Vine | Incomplete |
| KP215 Topics in Human Nutrition | L.L. Narwan | Incomplete |
| KP257 Cardiovascular Exercise | N.N. Rasmussen | Incomplete |
| SO459 Sociocultural Aspects of Sport | L.O. Wall | Incomplete |
| EN341 The Mystery Novel | D.R. Hemenhof | Incomplete |

"What do you think?" Devorkian asked after a time.

"His marks aren't as good," Hosschuk answered. "And what's this kinesiology course?"

"That's a fancy university term for physical education. It's the theory behind sports and sports training," Devorkian explained.

"He's a jock."

"Precisely. What else do you see?"

Hosschuk thought a moment. He's only in second year. He wasn't even at the university the year the first victim, Lorraine Malthus, was killed."

"Yes," agreed Devorkian. "Unless he visited campus. He's a football player. Maybe the university invited him to campus that spring as part of its efforts to recruit him for the football team. It's something we'll have to check out."

"Is that what we're going to do next?"

"No, next we are going to interview some more of the men who went into the endowment lands the night Pamela Wright was killed."

*****

Professor Henderson's bookshelves were packed floor to ceiling with books. That was not the case in this office. Here the top two rows of shelves were filled with gleaming white statues, many of them erotic. The man sitting behind the desk wore a well-tailored suit and had dark bushy hair and a black goatee. He smiled. "I have been expecting you," he said.

"And why is that?" Devorkian asked. He and Hosschuk were seated in chairs on the other side of the desk.

"Because I presume you saw me on the surveillance cameras in parking lot D the night that Pamela Wright was killed."

"How do you know there were surveillance cameras, Dr. Kingston?" Devorkian asked.

"Well, word gets around on a university campus," Kingston answered.

"Who specifically told you?" Devorkian demanded.

Kingston paused. "I believe it was a student named Tyler Tapinski," he said. "Why does it matter?"

Devorkian ignored the question. "If you knew you would be on the surveillance cameras, why did you go into the endowment lands?"

Kingston smiled again. It seemed a charming but humorless smile. "I wasn't doing anything wrong, so what difference does it make that there were cameras?"

"Why did you go into the endowment lands?" Devorkian persisted.

"Anthesterion," Kingston answered.

"What does that mean?" Devorkian asked patiently.

Kingston smiled again. "Anthesterion is an ancient Greek festival celebrated each spring. It is also known as 'Dionysus in the Bog.' It was a festival in which young men would travel outside the city walls and into the woods after midnight to mark the beginning of spring and the return of fertility. As you probably have learned, I teach classical literature. I find it interesting to practice some of the ancient festivals as a means of better understanding what I am teaching—to practice what I preach, so to speak."

Devorkian thought for a moment. "Dionysus is the god of wine, is he not?" he asked.

"Very good, Detective!" Kingston enthused. "Yes, Dionysus is the god of wine, and I did indeed bring along a bottle of wine—and drank from it. Dionysus also is the god of fertility and sexuality."

"So, you went into the woods to have sex with Pamela Wright."

"Certainly not, Detective. Anthesterion is a festival only for young men. I went into the woods to have sex with a student named Don Hamilton."

Hosschuk's jaw dropped.

Devorkian paused. "The football player?"

Kingston smiled again. "Athletic young men were preferred for the rites in ancient Greece."

"Isn't it unethical for a professor to have sex with a student?" Devorkian asked.

"It is officially frowned upon," Kingston agreed, "but Anthesterion was sometimes frowned upon by the authorities in ancient Greece too. It didn't stop the practice. It is a matter of freedom of religion. Besides, Don Hamilton is a consenting adult, and he is not in any of my classes, so he is not my student. In any case, I could hardly deny what I was doing since you caught me on your surveillance cameras and I want to be helpful to you in your investigation."

"Didn't the ancient Greek festivals sometimes include human sacrifice, particularly the sacrifice of young women?" Devorkian asked.

"You are well read, Detective," Kingston answered. "Human sacrifice was sometimes practiced, but it was not practiced in this case."

"So you didn't sacrifice Pamela Wright as part of your religious rites?"

"No, Detective, we did not."

"You were in the woods at the same time she was. Did you see her there?"

"I'm afraid not," Kingston answered. "We didn't see anyone else there. Of course, we were off the path among the trees."

"Could Pamela Wright have known what you were doing?"

"I don't see how, Detective. I did not know her, and I certainly did not tell her."

"Could Don Hamilton have told her?"

"I doubt it. Why don't you ask him?"

"Do you have any idea why Pamela Wright might have gone into the woods that night?"

"No idea at all, Detective. As I said, I had never met her."

\*\*\*\*\*

"I didn't see that coming," Hosschuk said on the way back to the car. "Did you?"

"Certainly not," Devorkian answered, mimicking Kingston.

"That Athenian thing—is that a real...whatever?"

"The Anthesterion? I have no doubt that a festival by that name existed in ancient Greece, and Dionysus is the actual name of a Greek god. But there's always a lot of interpretation in these things. Most of what Kingston said is probably academic BS, a theory he put together out of ancient materials in order to justify what he wanted to do."

"So Greeks didn't go off into the woods like that?"

"A professor and a student in the endowment lands at the stroke of midnight—I don't think so."

"Having sex with a student—can't he get into trouble for that?"

"Having sex with a minor is illegal, of course. Among adults, there is also something called professional sexual abuse. If there is a great discrepancy in power between two partners in a sexual relationship, it can be considered sexual assault. For instance, if a boss coerces a worker into having sex with him in order to keep her job, or if a professor coerces a student into having sex in order to pass a course. Counselors and doctors and priests are not supposed to have sex with their patients because their positions give them a great deal of control, making the patients vulnerable."

"That's what I thought. So we could charge him?"

"Not a chance. If Don Hamilton was a female, maybe. But he's a football player. Can you imagine trying to convince a jury that Hamilton was a helpless victim of that middle-aged professor? We'd get laughed out of court."

"But the university could do something, fire him maybe."

"If the university knew about it. It's probably a violation of the university's code of conduct. But the university won't. For one thing, Kingston would claim it was a violation of his academic freedom. And he would claim it's a violation of his religious freedom. And he's homosexual. He would claim it's an attack on his sexual orientation. He'd take it to a human rights tribunal. He'd fight it all the way to the Supreme Court. It would be a legal quagmire and a public relations disaster, a university persecuting a professor for his sexual orientation. Unless Don Hamilton lodges a formal complaint, the university will choose to know nothing about what Kingston is doing." Devorkian paused. "Of course, all that is assuming that he and Don Hamilton were doing what he says they were doing."

"You mean you don't believe him?"

"I don't know. That's why we are going to talk to Don Hamilton."

\*\*\*\*\*

"That is a lot of doors." Hosschuk stated the obvious.

The new brick building was on the south side of University Avenue across from the university and had ten doors across the front of it.

"You should read more," Devorkian answered. "There have been articles about this building in the paper. It has won awards for its innovative design—and received a lot of criticism. There are twenty-four bachelor suites on three floors, averaging six hundred square feet each, and each with a private entrance, perfect for discriminating students from superior homes."

"You're quoting, right?" Hosschuk asked.

"Directly from the promotional literature." Devorkian went up five steps to the fourth door from the left and rang the doorbell.

It took three rings before the door eased open enough for a disheveled head to appear.

"Don Hamilton?" Devorkian inquired.

"Yeah?"

"Mr. Hamilton, I am Detective Devorkian, and this is Sergeant Hosschuk from the Winnipeg Police. Could we come in and talk with you for a few minutes?"

Don Hamilton looked a little more awake and a little more wary. "I guess," he said. "What about?"

"Pamela Wright."

Hamilton looked even more awake and more wary, but he nodded and opened the door wider. He was dressed in gray sweats. The room behind him was new and bright and quite messy.

"This is a nice place." Devorkian eased into the conversation. "Do you live here alone?"

"Yeah." Hamilton was standing awkwardly in the middle of the room as if uncertain what to do next.

Devorkian did nothing to ease Hamilton's discomfort. "Did you know Pamela Wright?"

Hamilton shook his head. "She was in one of my classes, but I didn't know her."

"Did you ever talk to her?"

"No."

"What was your impression of her?'

Hamilton shrugged. "I don't know. She wore short skirts and heavy make-up. She was an okay student, I guess."

"Were you attracted to her?'

Hamilton shook his head.

"Why not?" Devorkian asked.

"I just wasn't."

"Did you kill her?"

"No," Hamilton said forcefully.

"Then why did you go into the endowment lands last Wednesday night?" Devorkian was firing questions rapidly now.

"How do you know I did?"

"Because you were seen on the surveillance cameras. Did you know about them?"

"Not then. I found out later."

"When later?"

"Friday."

"Who told you?"

"One of the professors."

"Which one?"

"Professor Kingston."

"Why did he tell you?"

Hamilton shrugged. "Because he said the police would probably come and talk to me."

"Did Professor Kingston know about the cameras before that night?"

Hamilton shrugged again. "I guess."

"But he didn't tell you? Why not?"

"I don't know. I guess because he didn't think it mattered until Pamela...uh..."

"But it matters to you?"

Hamilton shrugged again. "I guess."

"Why?"

"I don't know."

"Does it have something to do with the reason you went into the endowment lands?"

"Yeah."

"Why did you go into the endowment lands?"

"To meet somebody."

"Who?"

"Professor Kingston." Hamilton was becoming angry.

"Why did you meet him there at that time of night?'

"There was this religious ritual thing he wanted to do. Every year he picks one of the students to inaugurate the season."

"And this year he picked you?"

"Yeah."

"To inaugurate the season?"

"To mark the beginning of spring, so we could...There's this part of the woods where we...students...uh..."

"Meet to have sex?"

"Yeah." Hamilton looked agitated.

"You mean homosexual sex?"

"You're not going to publicize this or tell anyone, are you?"

"Why not? You're not openly gay?"

"I'm a football player. It wouldn't be good for my career."

"So you met Dr. Kingston in the endowment lands to have sex?"

"Yeah."

"Is that what you did?"

"Yeah."

"Are you sure?"

"Of course."

"You didn't, for instance, kill Pamela Wright instead?"

"No."

"Did she see you there?"

"No." Hamilton's eyes widened. "I don't think so. We were in the trees."

"Did you see her?"

"No."

"Did you see anybody else that night?"

"No. It was late. There wasn't anybody else around."

"Were you on campus in April two years ago?"

"What?"

"Were you on campus in April two years ago?"

"I was in high school two years ago."

"But did you come to campus to check out the football program?"

Hamilton was silent. Finally, he answered. "Yeah."

"Were you on campus when Lorraine Malthus was killed?"

"Yeah. I remember that. My parents didn't want me to come to this university after that."

"Did you kill Lorraine Malthus?"

"No."

"Did you go into the endowment lands during that visit?"

"No. I didn't know about...you know...the woods then."

*****

"What did you think?" Devorkian asked when they were back outside on the sidewalk.

Hosschuk shrugged. "Their stories agreed."

191

"Sure, but Hamilton admitted they talked on Friday. They had lots of time to get their story straight."

"Do you think they're lying?"

"Who knows? They could have done exactly what they said, but Pamela Wright saw them, so they killed her."

"But why did she go into the woods in the first place? Was she spying on them?"

"That's the question." Devorkian agreed. "Why did she go into the endowment lands? Why did any of the victims go into the endowment lands?"

"I have another question," Hosschuk said. "If Kingston knew about the surveillance cameras, why did he go into the endowment lands? Why not skip it for this year?"

Devorkian thought a moment. "I suspect he didn't care. Or maybe he did care. Dr. Kingston seems to me to be the kind of man who likes to flaunt his eccentricities. I suspect he enjoyed the idea of the police watching what he was doing. The risk was part of the attraction. On the other hand, if he got his information from Tyler Tapinski, then he probably knew about the twenty-four-hour cycle. If Pamela Wright hadn't been killed that night, the tapes would have been recorded over, and no one would have known he was even there."

"So when he realized Pamela had been murdered, then he knew he had to warn Hamilton. But why didn't he tell him before?"

"Maybe he was afraid Hamilton would back out of the meeting if he knew about the cameras. Or maybe he enjoyed knowing something Hamilton didn't. Kingston seems to be the dominant partner in the relationship."

"So what do we do now?"

"I've got some things to do. Why don't you stay here for a while and knock on the other doors. See if the other residents can confirm that Hamilton is gay, if he ever brought girls here or other men. Maybe they heard something through the walls. See what you can find out about Hamilton himself."

# Chapter 38
## Tuesday, April 14

"I got it." Devorkian said as he came into the office.

"Got what?" Hosschuk asked.

"A search warrant for David Horcoff's residence," Devorkian answered. "Anything else new?"

"Yeah. Mike Madrigal left a message. He says he has some things to show us."

"Okay. Let's see him first."

On their way to the video lab, Devorkian asked, "What did you get from Don Hamilton's neighbors?"

Hosschuk shook his head. "They market those places for their privacy for good reason. Most of the neighbors were home, but most didn't even know who Don Hamilton is. A couple said they had seen him at some time. Nobody saw him with anybody. And the places must be well built. Nobody heard anything through the walls."

"That's what the marketing literature says," Devorkian agreed.

"I'll go back later and see if I can find the rest of the neighbors," Hosschuk said.

They were at the lab. "What have you got?" Devorkian asked Madrigal, not bothering to give him a greeting.

Madrigal seemed to prefer it that way. Without looking up, he rolled his chair over to a side table and picked up a brown envelope. He wheeled back and handed the envelope to Devorkian.

"Four things," Madrigal said, holding up four fingers and looking at his fingers rather than at Devorkian. "First, the homeless guy. I can't see him on any of the tapes going onto the woods."

"So how did he get there?" Devorkian asked.

"The store's video surveillance is also on a twenty-four-hour loop. We pulled all the tapes a little before noon on Thursday."

"So, he must have gone into the endowment lands before noon on Wednesday and stayed there till midnight?" Devorkian asked.

"I guess so. That's for you to figure out. I'm just telling you what is and what isn't on the tapes."

"Okay."

Madrigal held up two fingers. "Second, the shopping cart. I pulled a shot of the shopping cart off the surveillance tapes, and we photographed the cart the homeless guy had. They're not the same; the design's slightly different."

"We searched the wrong cart?" Hosschuk said. "He had another cart somewhere else, one with the real evidence in it?"

Madrigal shrugged.

"What's next?" Devorkian asked.

Madrigal held up three fingers and gestured toward the envelope. "Guy in the leather coat. I got a close-up. He had a wine bottle tucked under his arm. He had the same bottle when he came out. It looks like dark glass, so I can't tell how full it is."

Devorkian pulled some photos out of the envelope. The top one showed the wine bottle. "What else?"

Madrigal held up four fingers. "The guy you thought was a janitor. I didn't see this before, but he had something in his other hand, the one that doesn't reach for the cigarettes. It was mostly behind his body, so I couldn't get a good shot of it. It looks rectangular or cylindrical, maybe about the size of a pop can."

"Okay," Devorkian said, looking at the next photo.

"The thing is," Madrigal continued, "he doesn't have it when he comes back out."

Devorkian nodded. "What about the other photos?"

"They're close-ups of the faces. Not all of them. Some never looked up at the camera, and there was no view of the faces at all."

Devorkian leafed through the other photos. They seemed to just confirm the identities they already had—of John Smyth, Don Hamilton, and some of the others. "Is that it?" he asked.

"For now. We still have a lot of details to look at yet."

"Thank you," Devorkian said on his way out the door.

Once they were out in the hall, Hosschuk asked, "Now what? We're going to David Horcoff's place?"

"No," Devorkian answered. "I'll go there with the search warrant and the forensics team. Why don't you go back to the endowment lands and check the path closest to the river that the janitor used. See if you can find what he brought in and left behind."

"Didn't we already search the endowment lands?"

"Just the area where we found Pamela Wright and the paths leading to it. We didn't do a sweep of the entire hundred acres."

"What about Sergeant Pepper?"

"I'm going to ask Constable Martin to put a tail on him and see if we can find that other shopping cart."

*****

Two police vehicles pulled up in front of a two-story house fronted with dirty gray stucco accented with peeling, dark brown trim. The occupants of the vehicles wasted no time getting to the building's front door. Devorkian pounded hard. He was pounding a second time when the door swung open to reveal a waif-like girl with long, blonde hair. She was dressed in a sweat shirt and blue jeans. She stood staring at the policemen without saying a word.

"We are from the Winnipeg Police," Devorkian said. "Is David Horcoff here?"

The girl shrugged. "I don't know."

"Does David have any storage space in the house other than his room?"

She shrugged again. "We each have a cupboard in the kitchen."

"Show Officer Branigan," Devorkian ordered and led the other officers up the stairs.

He knocked hard on the second door on the left. A few moments later, David Horcoff opened the door. He was dressed, but his hair was disheveled, and his eyes looked bleary.

"David Horcoff," Devorkian said. "We have a warrant to search your room. We would also like you to come down to the station for further questioning."

"Are you arresting me?" Horcoff asked.

"No," Devorkian answered. "We just want to ask you a few questions."

"About what?"

"About Pamela Wright."

Horcoff didn't say anything after that. He was taken outside and placed in the back of one of the cars.

\*\*\*\*\*

"I'm particularly interested in the backpack," Devorkian said. "Anything in that?"

Crassner, one of the forensics team, handed Devorkian a small book. Devorkian took it in his gloved hands and looked at it. "A Bible?" He opened the book and began flipping through the pages. Near the front was a Dedication page, with the blanks filled in with neat handwriting: "Presented to Meghan Hall by Charles and Sheila Hall, December 2004. 'Do not let this book depart from you; meditate on it day and night, so that you may be careful to do everything written in it. Then you will be prosperous and successful.' (Joshua 1:8)"

Devorkian looked at the page for a long moment. "Got him," he said quietly.

\*\*\*\*\*

David Horcoff was sitting in a bare room furnished only with a table and chairs. Devorkian came in and sat directly opposite him. Horcoff took a chair slightly to the side. Devorkian looked at Horcoff for a long time before speaking.

"David," he said softly, "we know you killed Meghan Hall, and now you've killed Pamela Wright. Why don't you tell us about it?"

"I didn't kill anyone," Horcoff said sullenly.

Devorkian reached into a briefcase on the floor at his feet and pulled out the Bible, encased in an evidence bag. He slid the book across the table toward Horcoff. "People who murder often take a souvenir from the victim. You took this Bible out of Merghan's backpack after you killed her, and you kept it to remind you of her."

Horcoff stared at the Bible. "Meghan gave me the Bible. She gave me the Bible before she died."

"Why would Meghan give you her Bible? It was important to her. It was a gift from her parents. The Dedication page specifically says that she should make sure she keeps it."

"She had another Bible. She gave me the Bible to read. She wanted me to become a Christian like her."

Devorkian smiled sadly. He said gently, "I find that hard to believe."

"I find it hard to believe too. It's not easy believing what she believed."

"That's not…" Devorkian started but then let it go. "Meghan didn't give you that Bible. You took it after you killed her—and you killed her because she wouldn't give you what you really wanted."

Horcoff said nothing.

"But why did you kill Pamela Wright?" Devorkian demanded. "For the same reason?"

"I didn't kill Pamela Wright."

"But you knew her?"

"She was in one of my classes, but I never talked to her. I didn't know her."

"Is that why you killed her, because she wouldn't talk to you?"

"I never tried to talk to her."

"Why?"

"I didn't want to."

"Because you knew a girl like her would never be interested in a loser like you?"

"I'm not a loser. Meghan said…"

"Meghan said what?"

Horcoff was silent, but Devorkian waited him out. "Meghan said that nobody was a loser, that everyone was equal in God's eyes."

"You were also in four other classes with Pamela Wright. Why are you hiding that?"

"I wasn't hiding it. That was first year. Those were big classes. I never talked to her."

"But you noticed her."

Horcoff glared at Devorkian. "She made herself noticeable. She always sat in the front row and wore really short skirts."

"Made you hot, did she?"

"I don't think she did it for the students. I think she did it to get better marks."

"Did that make you angry, that she wasn't interested in you?"

"No. I didn't really care."

"Then why did you go into the endowment lands last Wednesday night?" Devorkian demanded fiercely. "So you could kill her?" Devorkian leaned over the table into Horcoff's face.

Horcoff flinched. He stared at Devorkian. Finally, he asked, "What makes you think I went into the endowment lands last Wednesday night?"

"Surveillance cameras. You didn't know about those?"

Horcoff shook his head. "Tyler Tapinski said something about cameras, but I wasn't really listening. I didn't care anyway. I went in to think about Meghan. That's where she was killed."

"So you killed Pamela just like you killed Meghan?"

Horcoff shook his head.

"What did you do?" Devorkian shouted.

"I sat on a bench and looked at the river."

"For an hour? Bull! You sat there for a few minutes and then you got up and went and killed Pamela Wright!"

"I sat there for a long time. I walked up and down for a bit, and then I sat down again. I had a lot to think about."

"About how you killed Meghan and how you were going to kill Pamela?"

"No, I was thinking about something the old man said."

"Your father?"

"No, the old man in the class. Smyth."

"John Smyth?" Hosschuk interjected.

Devorkian glared at Hosschuk, then turned back to Horcoff. "Do you mean John Smyth?"

Horcoff nodded.

"When did you talk to Smyth?"

"It was that evening, at The Mystery of Chocolate. We went there to discuss a class project."

"What did he say to you?"

Horcoff composed himself for a moment. "Some of the professors say that there is no such thing as morality, right and wrong. The old man said that if that was true, then that would have to mean that there was nothing wrong with what was done to Meghan. But it *was* wrong! She didn't deserve to die."

"So you felt guilty for killing Meghan and went to the river to throw yourself in, but then decided to kill Pamela Wright instead."

Horcoff looked shocked. "I did think of throwing myself in, but I didn't—and I didn't kill Pamela or Meghan. I sat in the chocolate shop for a while thinking about what the old man had said. Then I went into the endowment lands and thought some more. That's where I felt I could be closer to her, where I could remember her. If you don't believe me, ask the old man."

\*\*\*\*\*

"What do you think?" Devorkian asked the usual question.

"I don't know," Hosschuk answered. "He could be lying, or he could be telling the truth. He didn't seem to know that the girls had been moved, that they might have been killed elsewhere and dumped in the woods."

"Or that's what he wants us to think," Devorkian said.

"What worries me more," Hosschuk continued, "is that we didn't find any trophies from the other girls, just Meghan Hall."

"So far, but maybe we will find something when we've examined everything in the forensics lab. Or maybe that just means that he cared about her more than the others."

"Are you going to check with John Smyth about what Horcoff said he said?"

"Oh, yes. But if it's true, there's one thing that Mr. Smyth and I agree on."

"What's that?"

"That there is such a thing as evil."

\*\*\*\*\*

Normally Devorkian would have preferred to see the face of the person he was talking to, so he could gauge the body reactions, but this time he decided to save himself the trip.

199

"Mr. Smyth," he said into the phone. "This is Detective Devorkian."

"Oh, hello…" Smyth started to speak, but Devorkian overrode him.

"What did you say to David Horcoff on Wednesday night at The Mystery of Chocolate?" Devorkian demanded.

"Well," Smyth said. "I said something about if there were no such thing as good and evil or morality, then it would have been okay for someone to kill Meghan Hall, but since it was wrong for someone to kill Meghan, then there must be such a thing as morality." Smyth paused. "Is that what David told you?"

Devorkian ignored the question. "When did you tell him that?"

"It was the end of the evening. A group of students meets every Wednesday night after class to work on a project. At the end, just he and I were left, and I spoke to him privately then."

"Then what happened?"

"Then I left and went back to my car to drive home."

"Where did David go?"

"I don't know. He was still in the restaurant when I left."

"Do you think he killed Pamela Wright?"

"I don't know. I don't think so."

"Thank you, Mr. Smyth."

"But why…"

But Devorkian had already hung up.

*****

"Hosschuk," Devorkian said when he had finished the call. "I forgot to ask whether you found anything in the woods."

Oh, yeah," Hosschuk answered. "There was a pop can, up in the fork of a tree. It was half full of cigarette butts. I sent it to forensics to see if they can get any prints off it, or maybe some DNA off the butts."

"Good thinking. Maybe the janitor was smoking with someone else. Since we found the can in the woods where the body was, it should be admissible in court."

# Chapter 39

## *Wednesday, April 15*

"Good morning, boss."

Devorkian, slumped in the chair behind his desk, looked up at Hosschuk. Devorkian looked as if he had slept little.

"Rough night?" Hosschuk asked. "Anything new?"

"No, nothing new," Devorkian answered, "and that's the problem. Forensics could not find anything to tie Horcoff to any of the murders, other than Meghan Hall's Bible."

"That doesn't mean he didn't kill them."

"No, but it means that we can't prove it—so far. I sent Horcoff home this morning. Did you pick up anything new?"

Hosschuk shook his head. "I went back to Don Hamilton's building and talked to most of the rest of the neighbors, all but one, and none of them saw or heard anything helpful."

"That doesn't mean he didn't kill them."

"No," Horcoff agreed, "just that we can't prove it."

"It's just like I said," Devorkian stated. "It's a classic English murder mystery. The surveillance cameras reduced our list of suspects to a small number. Pamela Wright was killed by one of the men who went into the endowment lands that night—David Horcoff, Sergeant Pepper, Dr. Kingston, Don Hamilton, or Michael Brown the janitor. The problem is that we just don't know which one."

"What about Don Henderson and John Smyth?"

"I would like to include them too, but I just don't see how they got into the endowment lands without being seen."

"Especially John Smyth, eh?"

Devorkian glared at Hosschuk. He was still glaring when a clerk walked into the office and dropped a large envelope onto Devorkian's desk. Devorkian picked it up and pulled out a report. After reading it, he smiled.

"This is the fingerprint report from Sergeant Pepper," he said. "They got a match. His real name is Sergeant Robert Peppard. Just over two years ago, he walked away from a mental hospital in Edmonton, where he was being treated for Post-Traumatic Stress Disorder."

"Is he considered dangerous?"

"Dangerous enough that they have issued a Canada-wide warrant."

"That makes him a serious suspect for the murders."

"He already was a serious suspect."

"What are we going to do?"

"I'm going to have Constable Martin pick him up."

"Then we'll interrogate him again?"

Devorkian thought for a moment. "No. I think we'll send him back to Edmonton."

"Why? Then we'll never be able to find out if he's guilty."

"No. We were getting nowhere talking with him. I wonder if the hospital if Edmonton, if they get him back on his medications, might be more successful."

"So what are we going to do?"

Devorkian nodded toward a pile of files on his desk. "Go through all of that again, the forensics reports, the interviews. I'm sure the answer is in there somewhere. We must have missed something."

\*\*\*\*\*

"But if you don't have a class," Ruby demanded, "why are you going to the university tonight?"

"I need to study for the exam."

"But you can study here."

"But there's a better atmosphere there." John Smyth caught Ruby's glare. "I don't mean better. I mean more intellectual." Ruby was still glaring. John fumbled. "I mean I feel more like a university student there, smarter..."

"Good. Because you sure aren't sounding very smart here."

"I know. Anyway, it's the second last night. The exam is next week."

Ruby sighed. "I don't like you going there. They haven't caught that murderer yet."

"But he only kills young women. He's not going to kill me."

"Alright. Just promise me you won't go anywhere near the endowment lands."

John Smyth paused. "Okay." He didn't tell Ruby that he parked in parking lot D. He decided that tonight he would park on the side of the lot closest to the university buildings.

*****

John Smyth had been sitting at a study carrel on the third floor of the university library for over an hour reading over his lecture notes. He didn't feel any smarter. Frustrated, he opened his briefcase and pulled out Meghan Hall's files that Sheila had given him.

"Sheila was right," he mused. "These printed notes are much easier to read than my chicken scratchings." Smyth flipped through the file with the notes Meghan had made on Professor Hemenhof's lectures. Each lecture was labeled with the date and lecture title.

Smyth then picked up the next file. This was labeled "Clues." Smyth opened the file and found a sheet of paper on which Meghan had typed out the clues for the bonus assignment. Smyth read them over again:

> 1. The eight of them often went on dates together, even though the relationships became a little complicated.
> 2. Rob was dating Laura, and his friend Roger was dating Bev, even though Bev would have preferred Rob.
> 3. Rob's sister, Mary, had dated Larry and Harry but decided she liked Larry best.
> 4. Larry was older than his brother and usually beat him at everything, but his brother wasn't like him at all.
> 5. Harry had a crush on Mary.
> 6. Mary and Alice often went to the ballet together and were out the night Laura was killed.
> 7. Roger was not related to anybody else in the group.
> 8. Rob and Laura had a fight. Rob stormed off, leaving Laura alone. An hour later, the killer struck.
> 9. Larry wondered if his brother had done it because he was jealous.

10. Roger was not interested in Mary, Alice, or Laura.

11. He killed her partly because he wanted to try everything and he wondered what it would be like to kill someone.

12. Larry was right although he didn't guess the whole story.

13. None of the men had an alibi, except Harry.

Smyth pondered the clues. He couldn't see anything there that he hadn't seen before. One of the clues, maybe number 11, seemed to be phrased differently in Meghan's list. It would probably take him a long time to find the clue in his own notes to check. He wondered whether he had really cared about solving the bonus assignment or if he had joined the study group just because he liked being with the other students. Or maybe he just liked chocolate.

He looked around for inspiration. At another carrel, a couple of students were whispering together conspiratorially. Farther away, a man in a well-tailored, black leather coat was browsing through the book stacks in search of something. He looked familiar, but it took Smyth a few moments to place him. Dr. Kingston.

Smyth looked back at the papers spread out on the desk in front of him. Maybe thirty seconds ticked by, and then something slipped into place. He slapped his hand down on the desk. "I know who did it," he muttered to himself. Then he began scribbling down notes on a piece of paper. When he was done, he looked over what he had written, smiled, and began pulling the papers and files together and stuffing them into his briefcase.

*****

"Is this doing any good?" Hosschuk groused. "We've been reading these reports for hours and haven't found anything. It's a waste of time. It's like studying for an exam."

Devorkian leaned back in his chair and rubbed his eyes. "Maybe you're right. An all-night cramming session isn't the best way to learn."

A clerk walked into the office and dropped a file on Hosschuk's desk. "You two still at it?" he asked.

"One more for the pile?" Hosschuk said. "What's this one?" He picked up the folder as the clerk slipped back out the door. "It's the fingerprint report on that pop can we picked up in the woods. It's going to tell us that the fingerprints belong to the janitor Michael Brown and we can arrest him for smoking or littering." He read a moment. "Or not." He sat up sharply.

"What is it?" Devorkian asked.

"The fingerprints belong to a man named Michael Barclay. He's got three convictions for sex crimes and served four years for rape. Got out four years ago."

Devorkian got out of his chair and went over to look at the file over Hosschuk's shoulder. "So, not the janitor."

"Yes, the janitor. Look at his picture." The photo showed a younger, thinner Michael Brown.

"He's changed his name. He's certainly strong enough to strangle four women," Devorkian said.

"But how did a convicted rapist get a job at a university?" Hosschuk asked.

"Good question. Let's go ask him."

*****

Smyth walked into the Riel Building and went up the stairs to the second floor. As he walked past, he noticed that Don Henderson's door was partly open and the English literature professor was sitting motionless in his chair, staring out through the window toward the endowment lands. As he reached the end of the hall, Smyth could see and hear the janitor vacuuming the floor at the end of a side hall. Dr. Hemenhof's door was partly open. Smyth knocked and walked in tentatively as the door swung farther open.

Hemenhof looked up from his work. He had been marking essays. "Mr. Smyth." he said mockingly. "Come to beg for a higher mark?"

"Uh…no…"

"Bribery is possible, but I doubt if you have enough money."

Smyth moved into the room and slid into a chair opposite the desk. "The bonus assignment…A group of us had been working on it…"

"Yes, yes, I have received Betty Borden's summary with your name on it. It was an adequate summary, but not remarkable. You won't be getting bonus marks. You don't get a bonus for working on it, only for solving it."

Smyth pulled a crumpled piece of paper from his coat pocket. He began reading, "There appear to be four men and four women in the story. According to clues nine and twelve, we decided that that the murderer was Larry's brother, so that meant the murderer was Rob, Roger, or Harry. According to clue three, the brother couldn't be Rob because Larry dated Rob's sister. According to clue seven, the brother couldn't be Roger because Roger is not related to anybody else. But, according to clue thirteen, Harry had an alibi."

"Mr. Smyth, all of that was in Betty's summary. As I have explained many times, you don't get any bonus marks for telling me that you weren't able to solve the puzzle."

Smyth looked back at the piece of paper again and frowned. "That means that there must be a fifth man in the story. My conclusion is that that fifth man is Bev, since Bev can also be a man's name. Bev is gay, since, according to clue two, he was dating Roger and, according to clue ten, Roger was also not interested in any of the women. This is confirmed by clue four, which says that Bev was different from his brother. Bev killed Laura partly because, according to clue eleven, he wanted to experience committing a murder. But he also killed Laura because, according to clues two and nine, he had a crush on Rob and so was jealous of Laura."

Hemenhof had not spoken or smiled during any of this. "Mr. Smyth, that is some of the most convoluted reasoning I have ever come across." He stared hard at Smyth and then finally stated, "It is also the correct answer."

Smyth's mouth dropped open. "So I get the bonus mark?"

"Yes, Mr. Smyth, you get the bonus mark."

"But since a group of us all worked together on this, that means we all get the bonus mark?"

"Did the group discover the solution or only you?"

"Well, only me," Smyth admitted. "But I couldn't have done it without the discussions we had together, so I think we all deserve the bonus. I've written the names of everyone in the group down on this paper." Smyth shoved the crumpled paper across the desk toward Dr. Hemenhof. "I'm sorry I didn't have time to type it up properly."

Hemenhof picked up the crumpled paper with some disgust. "You do surprise me sometimes, Mr. Smyth."

Outside in the hall, the whine of the janitor's vacuum cleaner was drawing nearer, and it was becoming harder for them to hear each other's words.

"You said only two other students had ever solved the bonus assignment," Smyth continued.

"Yes, Mr. Smyth, you are in elite company…or you made a lucky guess."

"Was Meghan Hall one of the other two?"

The janitor's vacuum was roaring right outside the door. Hemenhof got up, slid past Smyth, and pushed the door shut.

"Mr. Smyth, you really are more intelligent than you appear. You are correct again." Smyth turned to look up at Hemenhof, who was now behind him. Hemenhof continued, "Meghan came to see me here in my office one night just as you have done. She was a remarkably intelligent girl, too intelligent…"

And then Hemenhof was on him, his hands grasping for Smyth's throat. Smyth struggled and squirmed, slipping down into the space between his chair and the desk, just as he had squirmed out of the grasp of bullies at school when he had been a boy. Hemenhof struggled to regain his grip on Smyth's throat, squeezing down into the narrow space between desk and chair. Smyth flailed ineffectually to free himself from the grasp of the bigger and stronger man. The pressure on his throat increased. He tried to call for help, but only a strangled whimper came out. His head began to throb with pain, and his vision began to blur. Distantly, on the edge of consciousness, he heard a crash, and then a second crash. Air. Pain tore at his throat, but he was drawing air back into his lungs. He coughed. More pain. There was a weight on his chest, and he could hear moaning. Slowly, his vision began to clear. Above him, he could see the faces of Don Henderson and the janitor. Over Henderson's shoulder were more faces, faces he dimly recognized as belonging to Detective Devorkian and Sergeant Hosschuk.

# Chapter 40

## Thursday, April 16

"The doctor says it's just extensive bruising, and your throat will be better in a few days." It was long after midnight, and Ruby was sitting on the edge of John Smyth's hospital bed. She shook her head. "I told you to be careful," she added sternly.

"I guess I'm just much better looking than you thought," Smyth rasped. "Are you jealous?"

Ruby placed her hands on his upper chest and leaned her face down toward his. Her lips were just a couple of inches from his. "John Smyth," she said softly, "you are the most frustrating man. I think I am going to finish what Dr. Hemenhof started." Her hands slid upward. John Smyth's eyes widened.

"I don't think that would be a good idea. I'd hate to have to arrest you too."

Ruby sat bolt upright. Detective Devorkian was standing in the doorway, a smile on his lips.

"Although I have to admit there are times I have been tempted to strangle him myself." He paused. "Go ahead, Ruby. I'll cover it up."

John Smyth laughed, then grimaced as the laugh turned into a cough. "Detective Devorkian," he rasped, "you are not a nice man."

"I never said I was," Devorkian answered. "And you are a very lucky man. You almost became a murder victim."

Ruby shivered convulsively. "But what…?"

"I don't have all the answers yet. Dr. Henderson says that when he smashed in the door, he saw Dr. Hemenhof trying to kill you. He says his momentum carried him into Dr. Hemenhof, Dr. Hemenhof's head was driven into the desk, and he was knocked unconscious."

Ruby was about to ask more, but Devorkian held up his hand. "I haven't been able to question Dr. Hemenhof yet. He is down the hall.

Mr. Smyth, I would like to ask you a few questions, and then I'm going to talk to Dr. Hemenhof."

*****

"Any luck with the cameras?"

"I think so," Hosschuk answered. "The techs went through all of that footage we got earlier from the traffic cams and security cams. They got one shot of what looks like Hemenhof's Lexus going down University Avenue toward the supermarket about eleven-thirty that night. They're still working on bringing up the license plate. And there's another shot of the same car being driven away from the supermarket around one."

"What about the car?"

"Techs are working on it. They might find some hairs and fibers." Hosschuk paused. "Did you get anything here?"

It was late afternoon, and they were in Dieter Hemenhof's townhouse. Technicians were painstakingly going through it inch by inch.

"Not much." Devorkian paused. "There was a box with some lingerie in it, trophies, we think." He smiled. "And a box full of photos and videotapes, most of them date stamped. They include all of the victims, and some other young women we have not yet identified."

"All of the victims?"

"All but Meghan Hall."

"So you think maybe he didn't kill her, that it was a copycat, maybe David Horcoff?"

"No. Hemenhof killed her too. Probably in his office like he tried to kill Smyth— because she figured out he had killed the others."

"Why didn't she come to us?"

"Maybe she didn't figure it out until she was in his office."

"But do we have any proof?"

"Yes." Devorkian smiled grimly. "We found Meghan Hall's purity ring on a broken chain. The chain may have broken when he strangled her." He paused. "We found it in Lorraine Malthus's purse."

Hosschuk was silent.

"We also found some other things," Devorkian said.

"What?"

"Pamela Wright's high-heeled boots were in a closet, next to a camouflage jacket and a baseball cap."

# Chapter 41

## Saturday, April 18

"And he didn't say any more than that? He didn't say that he killed Meghan Hall or any of the other women?"

Smyth sighed and answered again, "No, he just said that Meghan had come in with the solution to the bonus assignment like I did, and that she was too intelligent. Then he closed and locked the door and tried to strangle me."

Devorkian leaned back in his chair and sighed. "Thank you, Mr. Smyth." Devorkian waved to the technician in the next room to turn off the recording equipment. They had spent the past hour going over and over Smyth's statement.

"We think we know how it was done," Devorkian said after a while.

"Pamela was already dead and it was Dr. Hemenhof who walked into the endowment lands in Pamela's long coat and a wig?" Smyth asked. "When I first saw the surveillance tape, I wasn't sure it was her, but I couldn't have said why."

"Yes," Devorkian said. "And then he took off the wig and coat and walked out the other side of the endowment lands in the army camouflage jacket and baseball cap. Then he got the body out of his car and walked back into the endowment lands with the body in the garbage bag in the shopping cart. He dumped her body and went back out with the garbage bag full of leaves or something."

Smyth nodded. "There's no doubt that he killed all of the women?"

Devorkian shook his head. "I can't talk to you about this. Let's just say that we found enough evidence in his condo to confirm that."

"You think he was having sex with all of them and he killed them to cover it up?"

Devorkian shrugged. "He seems to have picked one student to hook up with each year and then killed the student at the end of the year."

"Except Meghan," Smyth added.

"Yes," Devorkian said. "Meghan was the exception. We think she was killed because Dr. Hemenhof was afraid she had figured out what he was doing. But we don't know for sure. He's not talking. We don't know for sure why he killed any of them."

"I think I might be able to help you with that," Smyth said. "In his lectures, Dr. Hemenhof said human beings want to experience everything, even the dark and evil things…especially the dark and evil things. He said that was one of the motives for the murder in that bonus assignment too. Dr. Hemenhof said that there was no such thing as morality, no such thing as right and wrong, but he was fascinated with immorality, like he was addicted to it."

Devorkian nodded. "But that's speculation. We can't present that in court."

Both men lapsed into silence.

"You didn't solve this, you know," Devorkian said after a while. "You just happened to be in the right place at the right time."

Smyth raised a hand to his still bruised throat. "It felt more like I was in the wrong place." He smiled. "You're right. I didn't figure it out. Mehgan may have, but I didn't. But the point is not that I am smarter than you are, Detective. Or that I am smarter than Dr. Hemenhof. The point is that the truth was revealed and justice will be done."

"But that is not always the case. It doesn't prove there is a God. Not every killer is caught and punished."

"God does not make everything right in this world. He just does it often enough to prove that He will eventually do it."

Devorkian shook his head but said nothing more.

# Chapter 42
### Sunday, April 19

The Sunday morning crowd was milling around the lobby of Central Grace Evangelical Church. John Smyth was standing to one side, trying to see around people, looking for Ruby and the children.

"Mr. Smyth."

Startled, he looked straight ahead. David Horcoff was standing in front of him.

"Mr. Smyth, do you think it's true that Dr. Hemenhof killed Meghan?"

Hemenhof's arrest had been a headline story in local newspapers and news broadcasts. Details had been scanty. Hemenhof had been charged with Pamela Wright's murder, and police had named him as a suspect in the other deaths.

"Yes, David," Smyth answered. "There is not much doubt."

"Are you sure?"

"Yes, I'm sure."

. "But why would he kill Meghan?"

"Because he suspected that Meghan knew he had killed the other women. Meghan was very intelligent, you know."

Horcoff nodded but didn't say anything for a moment. Then he said, "Dr. Hemenhof is an evil man."

"Yes, David, he is."

"Thank you, Mr. Smyth." David paused and started to turn away, but then turned back. "I prayed that the killer would be caught."

Smyth nodded. As Horcoff turned away again, Smyth added. "And David…I'm glad you're here."

This time, Horcoff nodded, then walked away toward the door.

Smyth resumed looking for his family. A few moments later, as he looked in that direction, he saw that Horcoff had not made it out the door. He had been intercepted by Charles and Sheila Hall, who were engaging him in a stiff but intense conversation. Sheila was smiling.

# Chapter 43

## Wednesday, April 29

"Back again?"

Don Henderson was leaning back in his chair behind his neatly arranged desk in his well-ordered office.

John Smyth, settling into the chair on the other side of the desk, smiled. "I just signed up for Advanced Copyediting for the summer term."

"That's a good course, highly technical and demanding but good."

"That's what the lady in the registrar's office said. I'm looking forward to it. I hadn't been in school for a while, so I thought I should start with something relatively easy. That's why I signed up for the mystery novel course. It sounded like one of those popular culture courses departments come up with to attract students. Now I'm back into it, I think I'm ready for something harder."

"I ran into Bart McGwire the other day. He's the professor they assigned to finish the marking for the mystery novel course. He said he gave you an A on the major essay. What did you write on?"

"'Morality, Religion and Murder in the Chronicles of Brother Cadfael.' Edith Pageter had been writing murder mysteries under the pseudonym Ellis Peters, set in a wide variety of places with a wide variety of main characters. It was almost like she was looking for someplace to settle. Then she wrote one called *A Morbid Taste for Bones* about a twelfth-century monk in Shrewsbury. It was so popular, she ended up writing twenty more. She said that writing about a man of Christian faith forced her to think from that point of view and that in turn caused her to reconsider Christian faith for herself."

"I wonder what mark Dieter Hemenhof would have given you for that paper."

"Good question. I got the distinct impression he didn't really like me."

"I did warn you that university was a lot harder than Bible college."

"True," John Smyth answered, "but you didn't warn me that my professor might try to strangle me."

A heavy silence settled over the room.

"I wanted to thank you again for saving my life," Smyth said at last.

Henderson waved that idea off.

"How did you know to do that?" Smyth continued.

"I saw you go by my office," Henderson answered, "and it reminded me that I had seen Meghan go past my office too. That was what I didn't tell the police."

"Why not?"

"Because by that time the police already suspected me and were insisting that I had killed those students. I thought that if I told them Meghan had been on this floor that night, they would only suspect me even more and that would lead them farther away from the real killer. I had seen Meghan here earlier that night, but I didn't think that was relevant because, as far as I knew, she was killed much later in the endowment lands. I hadn't even paid much attention, and I didn't know who she had come to see. Then, when I saw you go by, it made me curious, and I started to wonder. I sat here thinking about it for a while, and then I got up and looked down the hall. That was just when Dieter closed the door, and I remembered I had heard a similar sound, of a door closing, the night Meghan was killed. I still wasn't convinced there was anything sinister going on, but I thought I would come down and check. When I got to the door, I could hear the two of you banging around in there. It sounded like you were trying to talk but the words were being choked off, so I broke the door open. My momentum half carried me into Dieter. I grabbed him and tried to pull him off you, but his head smashed into the desk and he just went limp. I didn't really have to do much."

"When did you call the police?"

"I didn't. They just showed up at that moment. I still don't know why. Maybe they were coming to question me again. I don't think they believed me at first when I told them that Dieter had been trying to kill you, but the janitor said that was true. They sent you and Dieter off to the hospital and questioned both me and the janitor pretty closely for an hour or so, separately, of course. At first, they were suspicious, but I

216

told them about Meghan, and after a while I think they started to think I might be telling the truth. One thing that seemed to make a difference was when they realized I had the same initials as Dieter, DH. I don't know why that mattered."

Smyth nodded. "But why were you here? When I enrolled, you told me you weren't usually in your office in the evening."

Henderson sighed. "That's true, but it was April."

"April?"

"Adrienne passed away in April. Most of the time, I can deal with it, but in April our house seems so empty I can hardly stand to be there. So I stay here to work…But most of the time I just sit here and stare out at those woods all evening."

Smyth nodded.

Henderson continued, "Maybe, in a way, I was supposed to be here, to stop Dieter."

Smyth was silent for a moment. "You know, in class, he even said why he did it. He said there was no such thing as right and wrong and that he wanted to have as many different experiences as he could. I guess that included having sex with students and committing murder."

"The ivory tower," Henderson said. "People talk about the university as a place for free thinking, a place where people can freely explore all kinds of ideas. Nothing is off limits. But you can't separate what happens in a university from the rest of the world. Thinking isn't free. Ideas have consequences. If someone says they don't believe in morality, I don't know why we should expect them to act morally."

Smyth was looking past Henderson, out at the endowment lands across parking lot D. Henderson followed his gaze, glancing behind him. "I'm not going to have that view much longer," he said.

"Why not?" Smyth asked.

"They're going to build a building there, the Pamela Wright Memorial Social Sciences Centre. Pamela's father is a wealthy mining executive from northern Manitoba and one of the university's main donors. Julian Randolph—he's the academic vice-president—convinced him it would be a fitting tribute. Randolph never misses an opportunity."

"They're taking out the parking lot?"

"Oh, yes. They're not going to touch the endowment lands, so they have to make the most of the land they have. They're putting two levels of underground parking under the building."

Smyth stared out the window. The trees in the endowment lands had a shading of green. The leaves were beginning to bud. Spring was finally coming.